THE Z-TEAM

Emmet Fitz-Hume had background. For generations his family had served his country in the diplomatic corps. Now he felt it was time for his country to serve him—with generous supplies of status and sex.

Austin Millbarge had brilliance. Even superiors who considered him a total slob had to respect his ability to crack enemy top secret codes with the help of a decoder wheel from a cereal box. Of course, it would have helped if he knew what the initials "KGB" stood for.

Fitz-Hume and Millbarge. Between them, even when faced with vicious enemy agents, savage primitive tribesmen, treacherously seductive women, betrayal from their own side, and imminent world cataclysm, there was nothing they couldn't do.

Nothing right, that is. . . .

SPIES LIKE US

More Big Laughs from SIGNET

SPIES LIKE US

Novelization by Gordon McGill

Screenplay by
Dan Aykroyd and Lowell Ganz
& Babaloo Mandel

Story by Dan Aykroyd
& Dave Thomas

A SIGNET BOOK

NEW AMERICAN LIBRARY

PUBLISHER'S NOTE

This novel is a work of fiction. Names, characters, places, and incidents either are the product of the author's imagination or are used fictitiously, and any resemblance to actual persons, living or dead, events, or locales is entirely coincidental.

SIGNET, SIGNET CLASSIC, MENTOR, PLUME, MERIDIAN AND NAL BOOKS
are published by New American Library,
1633 Broadway, New York, New York 10019

First Printing, December, 1985

1 2 3 4 5 6 7 8 9

PRINTED IN THE UNITED STATES OF AMERICA

— One —

For five weeks, since the morning it had been blasted out of the Cape into orbit, the NASA satellite known as *Hi-Weather IV* had lived up to the words stenciled on its hull:

NO MILITARY VALUE

But the phrase was a false declaration of intent.

Hi-Weather IV wasn't even interested in the weather.

Occasionally, in order to keep up appearances and check that the machinery was in working order, it would take snaps of cumulus in the Himalayas and storms in the Pacific. Now and again it would spin on its axis and photograph other objects in its orbit: a skeletal dog in a Soviet *soyuz*, gazing with dead eyes in bewilderment at the stars; a

blackened booster rocket; a line of plastic
bags, each bearing a stamp:

APOLLO XII—WASTE PRODUCTS
KEEP FROZEN

Nothing of interest. No military value
whatsoever.

Then on the thirty-eighth day, two hundred and ten miles over the Asian landmass,
it spotted something. From its innards came
a gentle throb of electronic indigestion. A
panel slowly opened and lenses automatically adjusted themselves. Took aim and fired.

Click.

A millisecond later, a color photograph,
seven-by-five, slid out of the incoming-data
receiver at base and a young monitoring technician gazed at it.

It was a portrait of a stag. A magnificent
beast, twelve-antlered, one foreleg raised,
snow on its hoof, staring upward as if posing.

The technician whistled. He knew one of
the guys who had built *Hi-Weather IV*. He
was an oddball. Now, looking at the stag, he
wondered briefly if they had managed to program emotion into the electronics. Maybe
the thing was bored up there.

Still whistling, he pinned the photograph
of the stag on his wall, next to the dead
Russian dog and the Apollo crap: what he
called his holiday snaps.

Deep in the forest, the stag's ears twitched.
It sniffed the wind, looked over its shoulder,

eyes bright, snout wet, nostrils quivering, then it blinked. Something had spoiled the idyllic morning.

It had no conception of carbon monoxide fuel that drifted toward it but it understood the smell behind it. Man had entered the forest. It was time to run.

A moment later the machine came into view, crushing pine and fir, spraying snow into untidy drifts, smashing everything before it.

The machine was vast. Ninety feet long, twelve feet high, four smoke-tinted windscreens hiding the crew from view. Six-foot-high wheels churned through the snow. Its cargo was sixty feet of steel cylinder meshed in green camouflage netting, a large five-pointed red star scarcely visible on its hull and a line of yellow-and-black arrows, the international signal meaning caution.

The giant machine battered its way over the stag's tracks and two men followed in its wake, men in white, their faces covered, only their eyes and nostrils visible, bringing up the rear, marching listlessly for there was nothing to fear in the forest. No enemies. No one within fifty miles.

Above them, unseen, lenses focused.

Click.

Click.

Click.

—Two—

The courier was a proud young man who boasted that he had never consciously given up any package that had been entrusted to him. He had lost only two packages. Both times he'd been hospitalized and he still felt deep guilt about his failures.

But his dedication had brought him to the notice of the state department. He had been recruited in a hospital. He had taken the oath. Now in a basement in Washington D.C., a suitcase was being handcuffed to his wrist. He would lose his arm before he would lose the case.

He clicked his heels and rode the elevator to ground level and stepped out, blinking into the winter sunshine. The fruit market was a rumble of activity, porters cursing as they pushed their crates and loaded vans.

The courier stepped out, looked left and

right. Above the door a sign announced in bold red:

ACE TOMATO COMPANY

The company truck was three yards away. But things could happen in three yards. He looked left and right, then strode to the passenger door, climbed in, and locked it.

So far so good. He rewarded the driver with a smile, knowing that the man was probably in awe of him, a respected courier, in charge of state security.

Slowly, so as not to attract attention, the Ace Tomato Company truck made its way through the bustle of the market, then picked up speed through the city.

Passing along Pennsylvania Avenue, the courier glanced at the White House and permitted himself a moment of fantasy, that perhaps the president was, at that moment, looking out and nodding to himself, secure in the knowledge that his most trusted servant was driving past with highly classified material chained to his wrist, the secrets safe.

They stopped in a side street in Georgetown. An expensive brownstone. The courier took a deep breath and checked the street. It was deserted.

So far so good.

Nodding to the driver, he opened the door and crossed the sidewalk, ran up the eight stone steps and hit the bell. It seemed like forever before the door opened, then he was through and being led across the hall and into the library.

It was rich in understated elegance. Paneled walls. Bookcases. A small, well-stocked bar. Two men looking expectantly at him.

He knew them by reputation. Ruby was a figure who inspired terror in the department. Only thirty, he was known to be ruthless.

Clean-cut, expensively suited, hair lacquered into shape, a Harvard tie, a mind, so it was said, as sharp as the creases in his pants.

Behind him, seated behind an elegant desk, was Harry Keyes. He was a legend. Nothing was known about him. The legend had grown in a vacuum. He had always kept himself to himself, but whenever there was a crisis, it was Harry Keyes who was rumored to have solved it. Sixty, gray-haired, and impeccably dressed.

Keyes and Ruby, the kingmaker and the heir apparent, looking at him and waiting.

The courier swallowed hard, and when he spoke, his voice crackled with tension.

"I have a priority package from the NATSAT printing room."

Ruby smiled. It was a horrible sight. "Why don't you say it a little louder? We'll open the window and you can shout it towards Moscow."

The courier mumbled an apology, and Ruby cut him off.

"It's not your fault you're stupid. Just open the case and get out of here."

The courier swallowed the insult. Mr. Ruby didn't mean it. He was under pressure. The courier understood. He understood pressure.

"The case is chained to my wrist," he explained. "And Security Dispatch has the key."

"Well then," said Keyes from his ladder, smiling, talking as if to a puppy. "Leave the material, take the case, and wait outside."

The courier was surprised. He thought they knew. But maybe they were so wrapped up in matters of state that they had no time for day-to-day details.

He shook his head. "No can do, sir. The material is locked to the interior of the case."

Ruby grunted in exasperation. "All right. Let's see it."

The courier slapped the case on the table, unlocked it, and watched them peer inside at the photos in their plastic sheaths, bound into the leather lining.

"Get in the closet," said Keyes.

The courier blinked. What closet?

In answer, Keyes reached for a book, pressed a concealed lever, and pulled open a panel. The books were false. Inside, there were cameras and sound equipment and no room to swing a cat. It would have to be an order from high up to make a proud young courier get in there.

Keyes pointed. The courier struggled inside, looking hurt. The door snapped shut on the chain. The young man had come to the end of his tether.

Ruby and Keyes crowded around the case and beamed at one another as they studied the photographs.

"*Hi-weather IV* submitted this stuff an hour ago," said Ruby.

"Beautiful close-ups," Keyes whispered, stroking the plastic with mottled hands. "Miegs and Sline will drool."

At the mention of the names, Ruby frowned. "They're late again," he said. "Unusual for soldiers."

But Keyes merely shrugged. He had dealt with the military all his life. Stupid people, but reliable. They usually knew what they were doing, and he said so.

On cue, the door was flung open and the two generals stood for a moment framed in the doorway, an explosion of color on their chests, ribbons like a fireworks display.

Sline, five-star air-force general from Strategic Air Command, built like a linebacker, not a trace of fat on him, a face that looked hacked out of marble then tanned deep brown. Mad blue eyes, staring at the two men as if they were about to be taken before a firing squad. An angry man, at odds with the world.

Miegs, older and shorter, a benign-looking three-star general from the U.S. Army Military Systems Command, was next to Sline. Ruby was reminded of TV soap operas, the good cop and the bad cop.

Ruby and Keyes smiled dutifully at them, both men well practiced in the art of concealing their true feelings. Ruby and Keyes thought of the military as dog handlers thought of their beasts. They were a lower species of limited intelligence.

In an ideal world there would be no need for men like Miegs and Sline, but the world was far from ideal. Military muscle was still an unfortunate necessity. The president and the secretary of state could not be allowed to go naked into the conference chamber.

And so, people like Miegs and Sline had to be patronized.

Together, as if reacting to a silent word of command, the two generals doffed caps and strode to the table.

"Are those the shots from the latest fly-by?" Miegs asked, greedily grabbing the case.

No time for hello or how're-you-doing, Ruby thought. These were action men.

"Right here, General," he said, perfecting his smile. "And they're beauties."

Sline sniffed and looked behind him. "Wait," he whispered. "There's someone in this closet."

"Ignore him, General," said Ruby.

"He's just one of our couriers," said Keyes.

A groan of deflated pride seeped from behind the bookcase. Everyone ignored it.

"Nice close-ups," said Miegs. "We're definitely approaching full-go hour."

Sline nodded in agreement and whispered, "I've greased the House Committee for Covert Appropriations. They think the funds are for more stealth bombers."

"I've selected two GLG-20s," Ruby said, when the chuckling had died down. "They're the best men we have."

"The last two were the best men we had," said Miegs, frowning. "Now they're the best dead men we have. I'm convinced that there's a security leak in your training program."

This was blasphemy but Ruby chose diplomatically to ignore it. He even offered a friendly smile.

"We could bypass training," he suggested.

"No," said Sline. "You'll go through training, but with four GLG-20s, two who are responsible for the project and two who are"—he paused and shrugged massive shoulders—"disposable."

Ruby didn't understand. "You're suggesting we assign this job to inferior personnel?"

Behind him Keyes tutted. He knew exactly how the military mind worked. He'd had years of experience. "No," he said. "I understand. Two teams. One to do the job. The other to be"—he copied Sline's gesture—"a diversion."

"You mean decoys?" Ruby said, astonished. "Targets?"

"Exactly," said Sline.

Ruby shook his head. He was still young. There was still a trace of morality clinging to him, just a hint of common humanity uncorrupted as yet by cynicism.

"GLG-20s don't grow on trees," he said, aware that his disapproval could probably be thought of as mutiny. "I hate to waste two of them as targets."

Miegs smirked. "I'm sure you can find a couple of men you won't mind wasting."

Then they were gone, leaving a smell of mothballs. Ruby shook his head. Not targets. He couldn't allow men to go out there into the cold without being properly briefed. It wasn't fair. Far better to appeal to patriotism, to ask two men to make the supreme sacrifice for their country.

He looked at Keyes. The old man was shaking his head as if reading his mind. No, perhaps not, Ruby thought. These were cynical times, requiring cynical decisions.

The last vestige of common humanity shriveled and died in the mind of Ruby from Harvard.

— *Three* —

The seventh floor of the state department building on C Street was a honeycomb of activity. Everyone in a fever, building careers, looking over his or her shoulder in case a supervisor was watching.

Everyone except Emmett Fitz-Hume, who was counting his blessings, feet up on the desk that he shared with Walter Jurgens in the southwest corner of the floor.

Fitz-Hume, by nature, was happy-go-lucky. Had he been younger and from the West Coast, they'd have called him something like laid-back. He was lying back in his seat, chewing gum, watching a mini-TV on the shelf at eye level. On his half of the desk, horror paperbacks competed for space with laundry bills and takeout menus.

Women liked him. He was gently handsome with a disarming smile, mischievous eyes, and a manner that suggested that he was secure in himself. Maybe his career wasn't going as well as it should. Maybe, at thirty-three, he should have risen higher than GIO. But he didn't worry. There was still time. He would be okay. Diplomacy, after all, was in his blood, and besides, he knew that he had an ace in the hole. Her name was Alice. She was his supervisor and a very good friend.

By contrast, Walter Jurgens, three feet away, was crisp, upwardly mobile, and heading for an ulcer. Conscientious, thought Fitz-Hume, to the point of insanity. But they got along. They were tolerant of one another.

Fitz-Hume yawned and adjusted the earphones that kept the noise of the room at bay. His half of the desk, he had once said, was an island of calm in a sea of turbulence. He liked the phrase. Said it often.

The TV showed an old Ronald Reagan show, *She's Working Her Way Through College*.

Fitz-Hume grinned, silently sang along for a few minutes until he gradually became aware of some activity on the periphery of his vision. He reluctantly turned away from the screen. Jurgens was making signs at him. By the look on his face, the man had been trying to attract his attention for some time.

He was holding up a pamphlet with the

state department logo on the cover and gesticulating wildly. Fitz-Hume silently offered him some gum, but the man wasn't appeased.

Sighing, halfway irritated, Fitz-Hume unplugged his ears. The clatter of typewriters and telex machines assaulted his brain.

He winced.

Jurgens tapped the pamphlet. "Aren't you taking this test tomorrow?" he asked.

So that was all that was bothering him?

"Foreign Service Board?" said Fitz-Hume. "Sure."

"Don't you have to study?"

"Nah," said Fitz-Hume, rolling his eyes. The guy was so naïve. "Are you kidding? I know that FSB test backwards. I've taken it three times."

But Jurgens was insistent. "They're supposed to be all different this year," he grumbled. "Five hundred questions in two hours."

Fitz-Hume turned away from the old Reagan movie, snatched the pamphlet out of Jurgens' neatly manicured fingers, flipped through it, and explained the facts of diplomatic life.

"Look at these samples," he said, selecting a page at random. "It's multiple choice. Easy." He flicked a finger against one of the questions and read aloud: " 'If discovered appropriating classified documents at a foreign consulate reception, you should:

" 'A. Express concern.

" 'B. Act surprised.

" 'C. Deny everything.

" 'D. All three.' "

He shrugged. "Answer D. All three. Of course, it's all commonsense stuff."

Jurgens was unconvinced. A hard man inside a bland exterior. "I guess you don't want advancement bad enough," he said.

Fitz-Hume tried for a hurt expression. "Ooooh," he said. "They don't expect you to know all that stuff." He sat up, looking dignified, tapping his forehead with his left index finger. "The important thing in the foreign service is one thing and one thing only—diplomacy, tact, and refinement bred into the individual's blood." He laid his hand on his heart. "My grandfather was an envoy. My father was an envoy. I was born into the trade." Then he winked. "Besides, I'm having an intimate lunch meeting with my supervisor."

"It's one o'clock," crooned a soft, eighteen-year-old, female voice over the P.A. "One o'clock briefing. We need three general information officers. Immediately."

"Aren't you up for the one o'clock?" Fitz-Hume asked.

"I'm right in the middle of this," Jurgens said. "Could you be a pal?"

"Sure," said Fitz-Hume, calculating the advantages. There was time before lunch. "What is it? The spraying issue again?"

Jurgens nodded and Fitz-Hume reached

for his jacket. A good deed for the day. Now Jurgens owed him.

In the elevator Fitz-Hume whistled softly as he rode to the floor where the media lived. He liked the press. They bought him drinks a lot.

The first briefing room was in use. A beefy man stood behind a lectern, his face bright from TV lights. Fitz-Hume glanced in as he passed and waved. The man waved back. His voice followed Fitz-Hume down the corridor, the catch phrase of the profession: "I can neither confirm nor deny . . ."

Fitz-Hume had been assigned to briefing room A9. He came in and smiled at the press. Ten of them gathered in front of the lectern, notebooks in hand. Three TV crews. An average haul. They stopped talking as Fitz-Hume came in. He felt a nice sensation of power. The messenger with the news the world was waiting to hear. Only *he* knew the answers. At least he would know when someone gave him the papers.

Cameras clicked. The spotlight was on him. Behind him, the Great Seal. In a booth, a technician switched off the Reagan movie and tapped his keyboard. On ten monitors Fitz-Hume's smiling face flashed up and the words:

EMMETT FITZ-HUME
STATE DEPARTMENT SPOKESMAN

Coast to coast.

The file was ready for him, lying by the bank of microphones. He plugged himself in, shuffled the papers, and spoke directly to the back of the room with no need for rehearsal.

"Gentlemen, as of this afternoon, the under secretary for South American affairs emphatically denies any and all intervention in the current realignment of top positions in the Paraguayan air force. Thank you."

He folded his papers, smiled a professional smile, unplugged himself, and turned to leave, but they wouldn't let him. They were on their feet, baying at him, waving mikes and ballpoint pens. A babble of noise. One voice clear above the others.

"What about the Paraguayan air force request for spraying subsidies?"

He was caught. Hadn't got out of there fast enough. Had to answer. Time to earn his corn.

"Spraying subsidies? Oh. Any visitors from Paraguay here? No?" He'd bought himself a couple of seconds to baffle them. "At this time, ah, in no position to bear . . . in any fashion whatsoever on the department for spraying the marijuana fields or for any subsidies due them under the current domestic aid agreements. Is that clear? Thank you. Good afternoon."

He made for the door again but they were on him, babbling and baying again. Fitz-

Hume sighed. Sometimes the public's right to know was a pain in the ass.

"How can you say we aren't spending millions on spraying," whined a man from CBS, "when the International Wheat Board reported contamination in the grain frields of southern Argentina?"

He was captured. Now was the time to do what his father and grandfather would have done. He tapped his mike and fudged.

"Well, it ... I ... Excuse me, are these mikes cutting out? I'm sensing a power cut here."

He fiddled with his earplug, tapped each mike, and improvised.

"The des ... yun ... commission ... plans ... or ... ow ... beyond their control ..."

The reporters were scribbling, trying to make sense of all this. The cameramen were adjusting their lenses. For half a second they were all preoccupied. There was a three-foot gap to the door. Fitz-Hume went through it and out into the corridor, slamming the door behind him. A close call.

Jurgens owed him.

—*Four*—

Across the city, Captain Hefling of the U.S. navy strode purposefully about his business, through the throng of tourists in the outer corridors of the Pentagon where the public could roam free.

Above him a woman's face flashed up on a bank of TV monitors, her monotonous voice filling the rooms with statistics: how many cups of coffee drunk each day in the Pentagon, how many pretzels eaten. Etcetera, etcetera. Some people wrote the information in notebooks. Others took photographs of the TV sets.

The captain walked with a seaman's roll. He had been shoreside for three years but he still walked as if he were bracing himself against the wrath of the Horn. Occasionally secretaries would snigger at him, but he paid them no attention. They were beneath his notice. Captain Hefling was a man's man.

He strode through Minuteman Hall, presented his pass to security, and took the elevator to the basement, then out and along the data-bank channels to a corridor marked SUBSUBBASEMENT D-25. Everywhere now there were warning signs:

SHOW YOUR PASS

CLEARANCE REQUIRED

UNAUTHORIZED PERSONNEL SUBJECT TO INDEF-INITE DETENTION

SENSITIVE AREA: NO OVAL PERMITS

C-GROUP ONLY

Hefling was happy here, away from civilians. He came to a door, unlocked it with a key attached to his belt, went into the boiler room, and clattered down a set of iron steps. He felt at home. The vast boiler room, thirty feet deep, reminded him of the engine room of his ship, and suddenly he felt homesick for the camaraderie of the service. Civilians knew no such feelings, he thought. They were pussy cats with no loyalty to anyone other than themselves.

He made his way between filing cabinets to the far corner. It was a mess, a junkyard of keyboards and terminals. Wires sprouted like weeds. A workbench was piled high with books and pieces of electronics. A mess. An affront to a military man accustomed to order.

Behind the desk, a man was reading a phrasebook.

Conversational Russian.

Hefling rapped the bench with his hat and the book was lowered, revealing an easygoing young man, a couldn't-give-a-shit kind of expression, smiling up at him.

"Millbarge," said Hefling, "where is the brain for the Scramjam 7000?"

Millbarge stifled a yawn and waved in the general direction of upstairs. "Procurement picked it up an hour ago," he said lazily.

"Well. Was it fixed?"

"Yep. New voice scramblers and everything."

Hefling was thrown off balance.

"Well then," he muttered. "What about that Red Chinese radio chatter?"

"It's done." Millbarge reached across his bench, picked up a piece of paper, and handed it over.

"Done?" Hefling said, staring at the translation. "That was a static-filled, triple-scrambled microwave transmission between two soldiers talking in Mandarin Chinese. How could you break their code so fast?"

Millbarge shrugged. "The Chinese used a simple twenty-digit square transposed in boustrophedonic form with multiple nulls." He scrabbled around in the chaos of his desk until he found what he was looking for. "I broke it with this."

He handed over a small plastic disc.

"A Drogan's decoder wheel?" said Hefling

in astonishment. "They put these things into cereal boxes for kids."

"Right," said Millbarge. "I got it from a box of Lucky Charms."

This wasn't good enough.

"Break it down again with the machines," Hefling said, striving for some authority.

"I already did."

"Well then . . ." He couldn't think of a way to impose his authority on this man. "Clean up the desk."

Millbarge smiled and with one arm swept everything off the bench onto the floor.

"There," said Hefling. "That's better." He turned to go, then looked back over his shoulder. "Oh, by the way. Good luck on the test tomorrow."

Millbarge lost his placid look. "Test?" he repeated. "What test?"

"The Foreign Service Board exam. Good luck."

"Foreign Service Board?" Millbarge said, suddenly getting to his feet. "Tomorrow? I can't take that test tomorrow. I haven't studied! I'm not prepared!"

Hefling walked away, Millbarge following him, grabbing his coat.

"You were bumped up on the list," Hefling explained. "You're scheduled for tomorrow morning. I'm sure I told you." He fumbled in his inside pocket and handed over a piece of paper.

"You graceless bastard," Millbarge roared.
"This is dated two weeks ago."

Hefling shrugged and backed away as the
big man came after him, his complacency a
thing of the past.

"You planned this," Millbarge said, reaching for Hefling's throat. "You want me to
fail that test so you can keep me down here
in the center of the earth doing your work
for you."

Hefling had heard enough, snapped back:
"You just watch your mouth, mister. The department is laying off civilians left and right."

Millbarge heaved on his coat, threw a scarf
around his neck, and grabbed the rungs of a
ladder.

"Where are you going?" Hefling asked.

"Home. To study."

Hefling laughed up at him. "One night's
studying for a grade-19 FSB exam? Good
luck!"

Millbarge kept going, shouting over his
shoulder, "Listen, Captain. I'm gonna pass
that test. And I'm gonna get out of this hole
and do important work for national security."

"Yeah, sure."

"And another thing." He stopped halfway
up and sneered. "I was gonna do your family
a favor and hook up the Disney Channel for
free. Well, forget it."

And he was gone.

— *Five* —

Lunch had been a hurried sandwich; a spritzer for her, a beer for him, nothing substantial. From experience, Fitz-Hume knew that you shouldn't eat or drink much before afternoon sex.

Three-course candlelit dinners were fine in the evenings, when you were actually going to sleep with the woman, but at lunchtime you didn't need anything that induced flatulence or made you drowsy.

Besides, they both had to be back at work that afternoon, separately visible so that there could be no hint of scandal.

It had been his place, this time, his neat little apartment in Capitol Hill. They were under the covers and the sex had been incredible.

He told her so. ". . . a really beautiful experience. Spiritual, uplifting. And I'm not just saying that because you're my supervisor, Alice." He wasn't exaggerating too much either. Alice was blond and green-eyed, did aerobics, and wasn't a problem to look at.

"I'm sorry about eating your diaphragm but I'm really glad you came over. And thanks for bringing clean sheets."

She smiled at him, amused, climbed out of bed, and started to dress. Fitz-Hume glanced at his watch. There was still time. He reached for her but she danced away.

"Shouldn't you be studying for that test tomorrow?" she said, her voice muffled as she pulled a sweater over her head.

"Well, I was thinking," Fitz-Hume said. "I'm not sure I really want to take that test."

Alice's head poked through and she frowned at him, perplexed. "But I thought you really wanted an embassy position."

"Yeah. I still want the embassy position. I just don't want to bother with the test."

He smiled his sweet, diplomatic smile but she didn't smile back.

"Fitz, you have to take the test."

He tried another angle. She'd spotted the fact that maybe he was being slightly devious with her, and if she thought about it too long, dwelt on it, then perhaps she'd get angry. It was time to play it straight.

"Listen, Alice, we've been seeing each other for months and have I ever tried to use our relationship to get ahead?"

"Constantly." The word was whipped at him as she pulled on a shoe.

"I meant today," trying for laughs. It didn't work. Her hands were on her hips now, which was a bad sign; it meant that she was thinking she was being used.

"Fitz, you have to take that test," she said. "And I'm very hurt that that's why you invited me over this afternoon."

He was in trouble and he knew it. He went for the big play.

"Hey, don't. Look, I'm not myself today. This morning I went to my neurologist, and, well . . ."

She didn't buy it. "You're not going to give me some bullshit that you're dying, are you?"

He shook his head, knowing when he was beaten. "Not now," he said as the door slammed.

He lay back, thinking of throwing some cheap line after her to regain some dignity, but he didn't bother. He wasn't too worried about dignity. "I'll show her," he said to himself, "I'll keep the sheets."

And with that comforting thought, Emmett Fitz-Hume fell asleep.

— *Six* —

Millbarge's fury had turned to constructive determination. He was going to show that jumped-up Popeye what Austin Millbarge could achieve in one night.

Captain Hefling had underestimated him. He didn't know about Millbarge's photographic memory and his high information-retention level. Millbarge was going to work all night. It wouldn't be easy but he could do it.

His studio apartment in Adams-Morgan was as chaotic as his workbench. The walls were decorated with posters from spy films: *From Russia with Love* next to *The Ipcress File*, with *Tinker Tailor Soldier Spy* sharing a wall with a color shot of the latest communication satellite, Hi-Weather IV.

As he gathered his stuff together—books,

coffee percolator, pencils, snack foods—he briefly indulged in a moment of nostalgia, remembering the day when his proud parents had taken him to an educational psychologist for tests and he had come out on top.

Abnormally high dexterity factor, photographic memory. Etcetera, etcetera. His mother had been scared. She didn't really want him to be abnormal. But his father was proud, talked her around, said the boy was destined for great things. His father had rubbed little Austin's three-year-old head and said one day he might even make president.

Now everything was ready. He reached for a pamphlet on Czechoslovakian surveillance procedures and settled down. He had calculated that he would work till five, get two hours' sleep, and be ready for the eight o'clock start.

The phone rang. Without moving his eyes from the page, he yanked out the cord. There was no time for phone calls.

A moment later, a knock on the door.

"Go away please," he shouted.

Another more urgent rap.

"No. I don't want any. Go away."

"Austin . . ." A female voice, young and pleading. "Please open up. It's Jennifer."

For the first time, Millbarge dragged his eyes away from his work, a slight frown puckering his fleshy features, a flutter of

memory tugging him away from the headquarters of the Prague security police.

He got up, opened the door, and saw a
vision. She was back-lit from the landing
light. Long, thick, shiny black hair, black
eyes. A fur coat. Long legs. Late twenties
maybe and walking past him into the room,
unannounced, uninvited and, right at that
moment, unwelcome.

"I'm sorry," Millbarge stammered. "I don't
think you have the right apartment." He
was sure she had the wrong apartment, in
fact. Beautiful women weren't a factor in his
life.

"I do if you're the Austin Millbarge who
went to Mary Washington College in 1972."

"Yes, I did. But that was fourteen years
ago."

"The Austin Mllbarge who made spectacu-
lar love one night on a desk in the Physics
lab with a young innocent co-ed named
Jennifer."

Now it came back. "Physics lab. You mean
the girl in Room 207 of the Goldstine Building?"

She nodded.

"It's you?" he squeaked. She'd grown.
"You?"

"In the lab . . . on the slab," she said, and
smiled.

Millbarge didn't know what to do with
himself, where to put his hands or his feet.

He could only babble. "You? Do you realize what you did to me?"

She nodded again but she had missed the point.

"I fell in love that night," Millbarge stammered. "It was the most incredible experience of my life. You said you loved me. You said we were going to be together for ever. I walked out of that room believing I'd found the one and only. I went to the jewelers next morning to pick out the ring. Then I tried to find you. But you were gone. I never saw you again. You disappeared and ruined all other women for me for the rest of my life."

"Well. I'm back," she said, and took off her coat. She was naked. A fantasy. The Prague police were no competition.

— *Seven* —

A cold Washington morning. Pedestrians going about their business. A few bystanders gossiping innocently about the weather.

A battered Saab drew up by the steps of a squat, anonymous building, and Emmett Fitz-Hume jumped out. He was wearing a patch over his right eye and a bandage on his left arm. He was shaving with an electric razor and running for the steps.

Behind the Saab a taxi stopped and disgorged Millbarge. He was white-faced and puffy-eyed from lack of sleep. His hair was uncombed and wild. A young woman was leaning out of the cab, grabbing at his knees. Beneath her fur coat she was naked, and shouting at him to come back.

"No more," he yelled, throwing money through the driver's window and hopping out of her reach. "Take her anywhere," he yelled.

A blackboard in the examination room was scrawled with optimistic words:

> Promotion Examination for Foreign Service, State Department and Department of Defense Employees, GS-10 and Above.

In front of it, leaning on his desk, the monitor surveyed his twenty-eight charges. Each had an exam paper in a folder, lying closed on each desk. The clock, next to a four-foot-square photograph of Henry Kissinger, read 7:59.

The monitor was thin, balding, and bespectacled, unprepossessing. He gazed for a moment at the ceiling, apparently daydreaming. A young man tried to take advantage and sneaked the folder open.

"Not yet." The monitor's voice speared the room and the young man blushed. A lesson had been learned. The monitor was not as dumb as he looked. He pushed himself off his desk and began to walk among them, then stopped at the door. They turned to look at him as he folded his arms and launched into a speech.

"These examinations," he said in a thin squeak of a voice, "are qualifiers for positions in the intelligence sections of our embassies overseas. The nature of your positions will be secret. Secret work is naturally very risky. Let me remind you what happened to one of our greatest Americans."

He paused. For a moment it seemed as if he was about to launch into the anthem, then he continued.

"An intelligence agent, operating in France, during the eighteenth century. His name?"

He looked around the room for a bright face but was met with vapid stares.

"His name was Ben Franklin and he sacrificed a lot. He lost much of his hair and turned asexual. So"—he smiled—"good luck. You may begin."

A crash and the door flew open, knocking the monitor off balance. Fitz-Hume and Millbarge were lodged in the doorway, each one trying to get in first. It was a standoff, then Fitz-Hume, ever the diplomat, stepped back with an "after you." Millbarge led the way in but Fitz-Hume was the first with his apology to the monitor.

"Sorry I'm late," he said, his charming smile firmly in place. "I had to be present at the reading of a will and couldn't leave till the very end when I found out I received nothing." He shrugged, held up his badge. "Broke my arm."

Millbarge tried the same smile but it came out a grimace. "I spent the night with a sick friend. Really sick."

Fitz-Hume took the monitor's arm, led him to the window, whispered: "Listen, I want to be comfortable when I take the test, so could you hold my wallet?"

He produced it from an inside pocket and held it under the man's nose.

"There's a thousand dollars in there," he said, and winked. "Or maybe there isn't. You know what I mean?"

The monitor whispered back: "Are you saying I can take the money if I help you to pass this test?"

Quick on the uptake, thought Fitz-Hume, but maybe it was a test. Fitz-Hume knew better than to commit himself.

"What do you think?" he whispered.

The monitor grunted an obscenity and turned away. Fitz-Hume shrugged. Nitwit, he thought. Didn't the man know that corruption was a way of life in the diplomatic service? Corruption and initiative. The man was a fool.

"Begin," the Monitor roared, and went to his desk, closed his eyes, and appeared to go to sleep. Millbarge and Fitz-Hume took their seats and flipped open the folders. Both men groaned. The others wrote fast. It did not look like a good morning for career advancement.

Millbarge could hardly keep his eyes open. Lethargy dragged at his eyelids, and when he blinked he thought of Jennifer. He had read all the books. He knew what lengths people would go to in the national interest. Le Carré and Deighton had told him. It was

obvious. Hefling wanted him in the basement for life. He had sent Jennifer to him.
Jennifer was working for the government.

There was a word for it. A sleeper. That
was it. Not that there had been any sleeping. Not a goddamn wink. He could feel the
scratch marks on his back, rubbing against
his nylon shirt. His very tongue ached.

Beneath him was a question on the Czechoslovakian security police. He yawned, then
became aware of someone coughing. He
glanced to his right and saw Fitz-Hume at
the next desk, winking at him with his good
eye and sliding a piece of paper across the
gap.

In large print Fitz-Hume had written:

WHAT DO THE INITIALS KGB STAND FOR?

Jesus, thought Millbarge, looking away,
trying to concentrate on the exam sheets,
but the coughing continued, louder and more
irritating, the madman with the eyepatch
nudging him now.

Millbarge looked up. The monitor seemed
to be asleep. It would be better to answer the
idiot's question and keep him quiet.

He wrote down the answer and slid it
across.

The eyes of the monitor peered at them
through slits. There was a standard procedure for situations like this. Surreptitiously
the monitor pressed a button in his desk.

Above the blackboard, two panels slid open

and two video cameras came to life, focusing on the scene beneath them, taking it all in.

For the next ten minutes Millbarge watched, fascinated, as Fitz-Hume went through his routine. He peeled off his eyepatch, stretched it as far as the elastic would allow, read something on the inside, and wrote it down, then winked again at Millbarge and slid the answer across.

Fitz-Hume was nothing if not generous. One good turn deserved another.

That done, he pulled what appeared to be chewing gum from his teeth. It wasn't gum. It was a length of grease paper, spotted with tiny writing.

Then he looked at the bandage, concealing a wealth of information, then at the soles of his shoes.

The two men exchanged sly glances and notes. The cameras took everything in.

— *Eight* —

Within an hour of the end of the examination, Generals Miegs and Sline were sitting in the Georgetown house with Ruby and Keyes, watching the antics of the two men on a video screen.

"Unbelievable," said Ruby as Fitz-Hume took off a shoe and gazed at the sole.

"I haven't seen shit like this since the Nixon administration," said Keyes.

"Who are these jokers?" asked Miegs.

In reply, Ruby hit the remote control and two personal files flashed up on the screen, with photographs full face and profile.

"The guy on the left is Emmett Fitz-Hume," said Ruby. "He's an information officer at state. Started there in seventy-four as a mail boy. Father got him the job. He's a snow-job man."

"And the other one?" asked Sline. "The one that looks like he's been up all night getting laid."

"Austin Millbarge," said Ruby. "Repair supervisor in DIA's code-breaking arm at the Pentagon. Wiggled into supervisor's pay through C-section. His last job before joining defense in seventy-five was fixing office copiers. Good with hardware. He's got some Russian."

Ruby looked at the faces of the military men for a reaction. There was none.

"Want to see their test scores?" he offered.

"What the hell for?" said Sline. "They're a couple of absolutely self-involved bullshit artists who've been caught cheating on a departmental exam. They'll do anything to save their jobs."

Sure, thought Ruby, but you need more than mere self-preservation and guilt for this job. He felt the need to elaborate a little, to spell it out for these two boneheads.

"One's got basic diplomacy skills. The other's a code breaker and has language ability."

"What more could we ask for?" said Keyes.

Miegs finally got the message. He beamed. "I say that's your diversion team," he said. "Smart enough to create a believable diversion and stupid enough not to realize their asses are in the wringer."

Sline grunted official approval. "I believe we've found our decoys," he said.

It was decided. Ruby winked at Keyes. All

that was required now was the interview.
Hardly necessary as far as the generals were
concerned but Ruby knew they would enjoy
meeting the decoys. Sline and Miegs, were,
after all, professional sadists.

He got to his feet, opened the door, and
called to an aide. A moment later Fitz-Hume
and Millbarge were ushered in. There were
no introductions. They were simply told to
sit.

Fitz-Hume had got rid of his patch and
bandage and was trying on his smile but
getting zero reaction. Millbarge looked as
though he were about to throw up.

Ruby didn't pussy foot around. He hit the
button on the tape and the *pièce de résistance*
of the exam room came on screen. Fitz-
Hume's moment of inspiration when he had
realized that he didn't have enough crib notes
on him to pass, when he had decided to go
for broke.

There he was on a twenty-one inch screen,
in full color and stereophonic sound, writh-
ing in his chair, choking, going pink in the
face, yelling to the monitor that the pressure
was too much, that he couldn't stand any
more of it, then lurching to his feet, gasping
that he was having a heart attack and col-
lapsing to the floor, grabbing the nearest
test paper on his way down and, in his ag-
ony, committing as much of it to memory as
possible.

Then there was Millbarge, seizing his

chance, yelling to everyone to stand back, saying that he was a trained cardiologist, demanding that Fitz-Hume be given some space and suggesting that the others leave the room.

It was inspired. Together they rolled on the floor, Millbarge fanning Fitz-Hume with a paper and reading the results as Fitz-Hume, in the commotion, copied down answer after answer.

The lights went up and the picture was frozen with Millbarge giving Fitz-Hume the kiss of life and trying to get information out of him.

"Seen enough?" asked Keyes, smiling, his voice kindly and avuncular. Millbarge wasn't taken in. He was about to leave the room and head for some tall building with an accessible roof when Fitz-Hume got to his feet and displayed the qualities that would one day, he reckoned, have him spoken of in the same breath as Henry Kissinger.

"That's not me," he said, pointing to the screen.

"What?" from Ruby.

"The guy on the tape," Fitz-Hume protested. "It's not me. Gentlemen, we've got an imposter on our hands. I mean, we don't even look alike."

It was a worthy try, Millbarge thought, but it had no chance. Four men shook their heads as Fitz-Hume babbled. The trouble with the guy, Millbarge thought, is that he's a romantic. Doesn't know when his tail's in a crack and swinging. He, Austin Millbarge, knew better. He was a realist. He knew that they were captured. Red-handed. No defense. No court of appeal.

"What are you going to do to us?" he asked, fixing on the nastiest face of the four men, the G.I. Joe with the suntan and the medals.

"A Section 384?" he suggested.

"What's that?" said Fitz-Hume, his composure suddenly cracking, the veneer of confidence crumbling to expose total terror.

"You don't want to know," Millbarge said, then turned to Ruby and Keyes. "Any chance of a one-one-six with D-12 privileges?"

Silence. A tableau of heads shaking.

Millbarge gave up. He shrugged his shoulders, suddenly bored by the charade.

"Okay. What are we going to get?"

"A promotion," said Ruby.

The two men blinked.

"That's right," said Ruby, soothing them, smiling. Suddenly all four men were smiling and nodding. "We're bucking you both up to GS-20. We like what we've seen of you guys."

This needed explanation and Millbarge said so.

"We're not recruiting for the Boy Scouts," said Keyes. "We want people who are aggressive, who know how to go after that little edge that you need to survive. And we especially like the way you two guys were working as a team in there. If you guys feel

you can work together, you're on your way
up."

Immediately Fitz-Hume was at Millbarge's
side, his arm around his shoulder, smiling
happily.

"We've got a very special assignment for
you," said Keyes.

"Foreign travel?" asked Fitz-Hume.

"Yes."

"Undercover work?" asked Millbarge.

"Yes."

"Free luggage?" asked Fitz-Hume.

Millbarge ignored him, reached for Ruby's
hand, and shook it, a dead-fish hand, blood-
less. Millbarge squeezed it and Ruby winced
but Millbarge wouldn't let go. This was what
he had always wanted.

"You won't regret this, sir," he burbled.
"I've been preparing myself for something
like this. I already know a man who can
surgically change my fingerprints."

"Yes, I'm sure you do," said Keyes.

Millbarge dropped Ruby's hand, turned to
Fitz-Hume, and introduced himself. Fitz-
Hume returned the favor.

"When do we begin our training, sir?"
Millbarge asked Ruby.

"Right now, gentlemen," he replied. "Welcome aboard."

Millbarge smiled happily.

Fitz-Hume's grin was a phony. Bulldozed,
he reckoned.

—*Nine*—

The aircraft was a C-141 Starfighter troop transporter. Any kid with a spotter book knew that. They were flying at twenty-six thousand feet. The altimeters on their wrists told them so. And by the direction and speed, Millbarge calculated they must be somewhere over Pennsylvania.

All these facts were easy. The hard part was to figure why they were sitting on a bench, wearing two parachutes, camouflaged jump suits, helmets, and boots; twenty of them, eighteen tough-looking men wearing the Flying Eagle of the U.S. parachute regiment—and Millbarge and Fitz-Hume.

The stench of sweat and fear was almost edible. Fitz-Hume was obviously terrified. Millbarge could tell by the trembling and

47

the silly jokes that the man was trying to
keep his spirits up.

Millbarge's balls ached. The tighter the
better, the guy in the hangar had said, as he
strapped Millbarge into his main chute.
"You'll feel more comfortable when you're in
the air."

A sadistic little joke. They liked their little jokes. They wouldn't make them jump.
You had to have training to jump out of an
aircraft. You had to know how to land properly. Stuff like that. No. It was just experience. To see the others do it and get an idea
what it would be like.

"We're just hitching a ride with these
guys," Fitz-Hume said suddenly, shouting
over the din of the engines. "They wouldn't
make us jump."

Millbarge tried for a smile to reassure him
but couldn't. The helmet was strapped on too
tight.

The sound of the engine changed, as if the
brakes were on, as if they were slowing for
something. Then lights started flashing above
them and a madman appeared from nowhere
yelling at them, a madman in a white suit,
roaring above the din: "Okay, sky troopers,
let's go!"

Sky troopers? Let's go? Where? Millbarge
thought, panicking.

In reply, a door in the rear slid open and
suddenly there was a dreadful noise of rush-
ing wind and the sky troopers were actually

paying attention to the madman, getting to their feet and filing toward the door with Fitz-Hume and Millbarge wedged between them, being carried along, pushed and shoved by the men behind.

Millbarge heard himself scream: "Wait, what is it? Where are we going?" The others had stopped but the madman was dragging Fitz-Hume and him by an arm each. "Why aren't they going first?" Millbarge yelled.

The trooper on his left nudged his buddy. "Sounds like they've never been on a HALO jump before."

HALO? What HALO?

They were at the door now, the breath sucked out of them. Pennsylvania or Massachusetts or New York goddamn City way below.

"HALO," said the madman, yelling in their ears. "Free-fall from twenty-six thousand feet to six thousand feet with timed 'chute release mechanism."

"High Altitude, Low opening."

Millbarge blinked at him. There was a yell. Fitz-Hume was gone. The madman had pushed him out. In that instant Millbarge's panic turned to rage. They had killed his friend. He opened his mouth to protest, felt someone's boot on his behind, then his rage turned back into total terror.

Silence. Complete silence. The only sound was his screaming in the slipstream as he fell, the breath sucked out of him, spinning and tumbling, the briefest glimpse of the aircraft way above him.

Fitz-Hume had fainted. It was a merciful release. He dropped unconscious from the height of Mount Everest through a thin cloudlayer, his altimeter spinning . . .

twenty thousand . . .

fifteen thousand . . .

ten thousand . . .

six thousand . . .

A puff and tiny explosion and the chute opened. Fitz-Hume awoke instantly and screamed. This was a nightmare. His body was being torn apart. His balls ached.

Then he was swinging gently like some fairground game. He closed his eyes and his life passed before him. He should have been nicer to his mother. He shouldn't have taken advantage of Alice's good nature. He shouldn't have cheated on the exam. He began to cry silently and for a moment he felt mistreated.

Hurled to his death for cheating on an exam. The punishment hardly fitted the crime.

He landed hard, jarring his spine, twisting knees and ankles, rolled in the dirt, the parachute settling gently over him like a shroud, then boots hit him in the back. He heard a thump and a yell, a voice he recognized. Millbarge had landed. On top of him. But it didn't matter. Nothing mattered except that they were alive.

They untangled themselves and unbuckled the chutes, stiffly got to their feet and looked around. It was dark. Some kind of forest. They'd been double lucky, Fitz-Hume thought. Could have landed in a tree, and what then?

"Where are we?" asked Fritz-Hume.

"How should I know? I lost track at seven thousand feet."

There was a squeak from the woods, something furry dying. They grabbed one another like babes in the wood. Then a howl.

"Did you hear that?" Fitz-Hume asked.

"Yeah. It's a dickfer," said Millbarge.

"What's a dickfer?"

"To pee with."

Fitz-Hume groaned and Millbarge shrugged apologetically. Terror was a strange thing; it retarded your sense of humor.

He was about to apologize when he heard a click up in the trees and they were blinded by a heavy-duty floodlight. Shading their eyes, they spun round. All around them, floodlights came on, turning night into day.

Center stage and bewildered. Then a scream. Fitz-Hume twitched. "Was that me?" he asked.

It wasn't. As their eyes adjusted to the glare, they saw a small man in black pyjamas and a black hood, fifty yards away, coming toward them fast, doing backflips and somersaults. Then he stopped and screamed again, adopted a fighting pose, the floodlights glinting off a curved sword.

"Ninja," said Millbarge, but Fitz-Hume

wasn't listening. He was transfixed. The terror had come back. Millbarge felt his heart batter his ribs as the Ninja went through his act, twirling his sword, slashing at the trees. Millbarge had read the book, Ninjas were nasty. Samurai assassins. But in Pennsylvania?

Swish, swish, and another scream.

Three saplings were chopped through and toppled, a creaking chorus bringing up the dust.

When it had cleared, they saw other Ninjas backflipping toward them, two from the left, one from the right. all with swords.

"We need a plan," said Millbarge.

Fitz-Hume searched for inspiration but found none.

"Let's play dead," he offered. Millbarge treated the suggestion with the contempt it deserved, ignored him, then turned at another screaming duet. Two more pyjama suits, a total of six now. They were surrounded.

"Come on, superspy," said Fitz-Hume. "Think of something."

"You're the diplomat. Talk to them." They were irritable with one another now, terror-stricken for the second time in a matter of minutes.

The Ninjas closed in. Fitz-Hume tried a grin, held up both hands in mock surrender. "All right," he shouted, striving for a tone of authority. "Stop right there and I'll bring back the sun."

They kept coming.

Fitz-Hume took a breath, thought of something, reached into his wallet jacket for his wallet.

"Okay, okay," he said fumbling for a photograph and holding it up, turning on one heel so they could all see. "This is my sister. You can all have her. I hear she's good."

Millbarge grunted in contempt, bent and picked up a fallen branch. He knew what to do. He was of all-American stock. He'd seen *The Alamo*.

"First one to take another step," he roared, "I'll split his head open."

"You hear that?" said Fitz-Hume to the Ninjas, suddenly seeing a way out. "He's threatening us. Let's get him." He grabbed at Millbarge's throat but missed.

"Show some balls," said Millbarge, dancing away.

"I think it's too late to impress them." Always the bad jokes, Millbarge thought. Fitz-Hume's flippancy would be the death of him.

The Ninjas were only a few yards away now, arms raised, their swords held double-fisted. They smelled awful. Two more paces, thought Millbarge, and it's kebab time.

Then they stopped, more lights beamed in on them from behind. They all turned to see a group of army jeeps. Soldiers watching impassively.

It was like the old movies again. Saved in the nick of time by the seventh cavalry.

Millbarge felt himself go weak at the knees as he watched his savior step out of the leading jeep and walk toward them—an enormous soldier, very black, wearing fatigues and a U.S. Rangers beret and carrying a clipboard. He stopped and nodded at the Ninjas.

"That's enough," he said.

Very curious. Millbarge dropped his twig and waited.

"Austin Millbarge?" said the soldier.

Millbarge snapped to attention with a "Here, sir."

The soldier ticked his board.

"Emmett Fitz-Hume?"

"Hi."

Another tick, then the soldier nodded. "Colonel Rhombus," he said sternly, no trace of friendship in his manner. "GS-20 training center. We've been expecting you."

"What was all this?" Millbarge wanted to know, pointing to the Ninjas.

"This is the way I welcome all new trainees."

'What's wrong with a hot cup of coffee and a handshake?" asked Fitz-Hume.

The colonel was unamused. "It's my job," he said slowly, "to prepare you to go out in the field. I like to find out as quickly as possible what I've got to work with." He tapped his clipboard. "I've already made my evaluation."

Millbarge's curiosity once more got the better of him. He peeked.

"What did he write?" whispered Fitz-Hume.

"Pussy."

Fitz-Hume was insulted. "I don't think that's fair," he told Rhombus, standing hands on hips like Alice when she was mad. "These guys had swords. What were we supposed to do?"

"It depends upon your particular area of combat," Rhombus replied. "Maybe this . . ."

His left leg snapped up and out, his boot catching the nearest Ninja in the throat. He whirled and karate-chopped a second on the collarbone. A snap and a scream. A kick here, a punch there, and the Ninjas were groveling and groaning.

It was fast. Blink and you'd have missed it.

"Come on," said Rhombus, "I'll take you back to the base." He hadn't broken a sweat or lost breath. There had been no time. Meekly Millbarge and Fitz-Hume followed him and for once Fitz-Hume swallowed a funny line, thought better of it.

On the way to the camp, bumping over ruts in the forest, they tried to concentrate on what Rhombus was saying. They were to be trained for a special collection, he told them. Normally he had a few months to train people but they had been sent on a special rush order. Next day they were going to go through a normal six months' training period to be ready for traveling by what he called twenty-three hundred.

They tried to take it in but it was too much for them. The adrenaline had ceased pumping, leaving a lethargic residue in their blood. They were given two camp beds and they were asleep almost as they hit the canvas.

Fitz-Hume dreamed of his father and in his dream he cursed the old man for skimping on the facts-of-life lecture. If only he had known more about the Alices of this world, he wouldn't be in this mess. No proper gigolo would have made such a mess of things.

Millbarge dreamed of Jennifer and of the deviousness of Captain Hefler and in his dream he couldn't make up his mind whether or not she had been worth it. . . .

—Ten—

They had been made to dress like soldiers—helmets and fatigues, boots that didn't fit, and they had been marched to the edge of a rectangular bog.

Mud and slime bubbled and swelled around their boots. A sulfurous stench made them gag. The bog reminded Fitz-Hume of their breakfast and he felt sick. His balls still ached from the parachute. He glanced at Millbarge. The big man couldn't grumble. He had virtually volunteered. He'd always wanted to make a career in the service, to do important work for national security, so maybe he wasn't feeling so bad about all this crap.

As for Emmett Fitz-Hume, third generation envoy, he didn't want to know. Kissinger never went through shit like this. They didn't make Kissinger's balls ache. Not literally anyway.

And now this lunatic Rhombus was pointing to the bog and talking garbage.

"This is your standard bog-negotiation trial," he drawled. "You will be judged on survivabiltty and speed. You are allotted two minutes, seventeen seconds. Enter NOW!"

This was ridiculous. They shook their heads. What was the point?

Rhombus fired a pistol in the air. They clamped their hands over their ears and edged away from the bog. It was a wrong move. Rhombus roared. "ENTER NOW!"

No. This was crazy, expecting them to wallow like goddamn hippos in a stinking bog. Fitz-Hume was trying to work out the rationale. In a few years' time he would be face-to-face with Gromyko or his successor, sorting out the world's problems. What advantage would a background of bog floundering give him in the negotiating chamber?

Millbarge was thinking along the same lines. He had once taken a Boy Scout orienteering course, designed to build character, and as far as character building was concerned, that was enough for one lifetime.

No. Hell. They wouldn't do it.

Rhombus aimed, fired at their feet. A millisecond later they were in the bog, having made racing dives worthy of Mark Spitz. Their helmets and boots kept them under, eating slime—in their mouths, up their nostrils, in their eyes and ears.

The lunatic Rhombus's words vaguely penetrated their sodden brains. "Survivability and speed."

What Rhombus should have said was, the faster you got out, the more chance you had to survive.

They spluttered to the surface, spewing sulfur through their teeth.

Through the muck that clung to their eyelids they could see six Rangers and Rhombus aiming guns at their heads. Through the slime in their ears they could hear the madman's voice yelling at them: "Heads down!"

Then the sound of automatic pistols and the lead hornets buzzing around their helmets.

And they went down again, instinctively, as deep as they could, deep in the shit, a hellish place to die. . . .

Five minutes later, stinking like badgers, they were standing in a field gazing at an obstacle course, at a field full of insanity. There were climbing bars, with tires attached, hanging over water, great big perpendicular walls with spikes.

Millbarge was well read. It was the Inquisition *al fresco*.

"This is your obstacle course," Rhombus was saying. "It is essentially the course familiar to armed service recruits except that here in intelligence-operative training, we

do it a bit differently. We add the element of
scorched earth."

On cue, something blew up on the course
and a couple of soldiers dived for cover. Then
something else. Incoming shells. Tracers,
flares, the sound of gunfire.

They could see the course clearly mapped
out in big numbers, one to ten, and they
were off and running, stinking the place out.
On the second item, something blew up and
a soldier grunted.

Millbarge looked back. The man seemed
to be bleeding from the mouth. It was amazing, he thought, what could be done with
makeup these days.

For an hour that seemed like a week
they threw themselves over walls, squirmed
through tires, threw knives at pop-up cardboard soldiers, while all around them, bullets whined and things kept exploding.

By the time they had finished the course,
they were dazed, bleeding from small cuts,
bruised all over, and deaf.

By the time they reached a lake, they no
longer cared what happened to them. Rhombus was standing in front of them, shouting
instructions.

Millbarge had taken a course in lipreading
and he managed to understand what the big
man wanted them to do. Something about
stepping into the water and attaching ropes
to their wrists. The ropes were tough and
chafed them. Millbarge looked across the lake.

Ten yards away, a man in a motorboat was grinning at them, sadistically it seemed.

Then Rhombus's mouth was opening and shutting again, something about verifying their ability to stay afloat at high speeds.

Millbarge was trying to translate to Fitz-Hume when the motorboat's engine roared and he was dragged off his feet, his arms almost loosened from their sockets, and he was swallowing water.

Water in his ears, nose and throat, water in his lungs. Highspeed water. Water at forty knots.

They were trying to drown him, like some unwanted kitten.

Emmett Fitz-Hume had always prided himself on his tolerance. He was blessed by a tolerant nature. And patience. Miles of patience. But by two o'clock—or what these fools referred to as fourteen hundred hours—he had run out of both qualities.

Maybe he had deluded himself over the years, but no matter. Self-analysis was a luxury when every bone ached and terror was corroding your brain.

He'd had enough. He was even prepared to go back to Washington in disgrace. He was prepared to resign before being fired and find himself some disreputable job; in public relations maybe; or, if the worst came to the worst, in journalism. But that was the future. All he needed now was a shower, three martinis, and Alice.

Millbarge agreed. He'd had enough. His ambition had died in him. He was a sadder but wiser man.

They found Rhombus outside a hangar, sipping ersatz coffee.

"Colonel," said Fitz-Hume, ever the spokesman.

"Yes?"

"We were just talking and this has been oodles of fun. I mean, we've made new friends, and lunch was great." He turned to his colleague for support. "Wasn't that great?"

"The tuna casserole," said Millbarge. "Unbelievable."

Nothing from Rhombus. They might as well have been talking to the hangar wall.

"Anyhow," said Fitz-Hume, "we were just talking and we'd like to go home now. So thanks for the bruises and you can keep the stool samples."

They turned away and were stabbed in the back by a sentence from Rhombus.

"Gentlemen, it would be a shame for me to kill you now."

They turned again and gazed at him. Rhombus walked off, ignoring them. For a moment Fitz-Hume watched him go, then turned to Millbarge, who was sitting, white-faced, arms wrapped around him as if in shock, in the position known to psychiatrists as fetal terror.

"What did he mean by that?" Fitz-Hume
asked.

"He means we're OIO," said Millbarge.

OIO? Fitz-Hume wondered. Some kind of
crossword clue?

"Obligated Involuntary Officers," Millbarge
whispered.

"Ah," said Fitz-Hume. It took him a moment to translate into street English but
when he did, he felt sick.

It had been the worst time of their lives.
No question. Millbarge had tried to dredge
from his memory all the nasty things that
had ever happened to him, physically and
mentally: the time he had fallen off his bike
and broken his wrist, the horrors of summer
camp in Poughkeepsie, the rejection by Bette-
Jane in front of the whole class . . .

Etcetera, etcetera.

But added together, mashed into a mental
meatball of horrendous experience, the memory was nothing compared to just one minute of the past three hours.

They called it AFPSR.

Air Force Passive Strain Response. At first,
from what Rhombus told them, it seemed
that it was going to be gentle and relaxing.
They would not be required to exert themselves at all. Sometimes they could even sit
down.

The first test was known as aggravated
body temperature measurement. They were

zipped into heavy-duty asbestos suits. Helmets were placed over their heads and shoulders and they were led to a wall.

Millbarge felt like Neil Armstrong being taken before a firing squad, and when he peered through the perspex slits in the helmet, he realized his imagination hadn't been far off the mark.

Rhombus was standing ten yards away, pointing a water hose at them. Except it wasn't water. There was a whoosh and they were hit by flames.

They were being roasted. They turned away toward the wall and danced, trying to keep their feet off the scorching tarmac. It seemed to go on forever. It was a foretaste of hell. Any second now, Fitz-Hume reckoned, somebody would pour barbecue sauce on them.

But they got through without fainting, leaving seven pounds of themselves in perspiration inside the suits.

Thinner, sweating, they were taken to the top of a forty-foot scaffolding and made to climb into the cockpit of a small single-engine aircraft. It was a T-38. Any schoolboy knew that. The only difference was that T-38s normally had wings. This had only a battered fuselage.

They were strapped in and given crash helmets. They looked down, saw Rhombus gazing up at them. He was tiny from their point of view, no more than an inch tall, yet he still looked menacing. He was holding a bullhorn to his lips and yelling:

"Crash simulation. Vertical impact."

Fitz-Hume liked playing the pilot. It was fun. He gave the thumbs-up to Millbarge and winked.

Anchors aweigh.

The world tilted, the horizon vanished. The concrete came up to meet them. The concussion blasted the breath out of them and every bone rattled. The fuselage broke up and they could see the sky, and Rhombus's face, full-size now, looking at them through the shattered cockpit and nodding. . . .

By five that afternoon they were in a state of shock. They no longer cared what Rhombus did to them. Maybe killing them earlier hadn't been so bad an idea after all.

"Boys, it would be a shame for me to kill you now," he had said.

Maybe.

They were strapped into a glass cockpit now, inside the hangar. It was comfortable. Nice leather seats, a cozy leather harness. Air conditioning even. They could see Rhombus ten yards away in a glass booth standing behind a console, looking like a sound engineer. Fitz-Hume fantasized. Maybe they'd give them microphones. Maybe they wanted to hear how well they could sing.

Rhombus's voice boomed through a speaker in the side of the cockpit: "Centrifugally stimulated brain monitoring."

And the cockpit began to spin. Slowly at first, not unpleasant, then quicker. Nausea set in. They could no longer see Rhombus. His face was a blur, then vanished altogether. All they could see was glass. A whiteout. Their bodies were forced deeper into the leather. Their mouths were dragged into a rictus grin. Their eyelids were sucked back into their skulls. Flesh quivered. They knew now that they were going to die and they could only hope that it would be quick.

In the tower Rhombus glanced at the dancing needles on the clock faces. Three hundred miles an hour. A G-force of ten.

He nodded. Enough. A technician pressed a button and put an end to their misery.

Ten minutes later they were led by a soldier into the command headquarters. They walked stiff-legged, side by side, bug-eyed, their faces set in a Halloween horror mask from the centrifuge. Soldiers who passed them paid them no attention. The soldiers were hardened, brutalized men who were accustomed to seeing gargoyle faces and thinking nothing of it.

Colonel Rhombus had a small tidy office. He sat behind a desk, his shoulders filling the room. Fitz-Hume and Millbarge stood stiffly by the door, at attention. They had no choice. They no longer had any control over their limbs.

The colonel looked at them and sniffed.

Millbarge waited, wondering what was coming next. Then Rhombus came up with the very last word he had expected:

"Congratulations."

Rhombus leaned back and nodded at them. "You are about to enter the operational phase of your assignment. I am not authorized to give you the complete operational package. However, I can tell you that the location of your initial drop will be well inside the borders of Pakistan."

"Pakistan?" they said as one, spraying him with spittle, the word from their distorted mouths like a parrot's squawk.

Pakistan ? Why Pakistan ? Then they thought, why not? Anywhere would be better than this place. It was something else he had said that bothered them; the word *drop*. At the thought of another parachute, Millbarge's palms began to sweat. Fitz-Hume's reaction was even more extreme.

In the confines of the small room, Rhombus noticed immediately. His nostrils flared in disgust and he told them to get the hell out.

Pakistan.

Fitz-Hume as he stiff-legged it to the men's room, tried to figure why Pakistan. There was nothing happening in Pakistan, wasn't there?

—Eleven—

The aluminium shipping container was ten feet long by four feet wide and four feet deep. Two-foot letters in red proclaimed that it was the property of the Ace Tomato Company. A two-foot diameter tomato wore a cheery smile.

The container could have shipped an orgy of tomatoes into the Pakistan desert. Instead it was dropping Millbarge and Fitz-Hume.

They had screamed again as they felt themselves fall, then they stopped. Screaming did you no good, and besides, the container had terrible acoustics. Their screams echoed and fed on themselves and so they contented themselves with whimpering as it dropped slowly, swinging gently through two thousand feet of clear blue sky.

They had been issued with combat fatigues

and kepis with sun flaps. Fitz-Hume, when he had tried his on, thought of *Beau Geste;* except he didn't look like Gary Cooper. He had looked more like Gary Cooper when his face had been ravaged by the centrifuge. Now he looked merely comical.

On the way down they slurped beer from a can, chewed pretzels, and wondered what they would find when they landed. Millbarge had been thinking. A six-month training course crammed into a day was meaningless, just a case of the military men covering themselves, so that, in case of failure, they could produce a memo saying that the deceased, Fitz-Hume and Millbarge, had passed through their hands and had been declared trained for the job.

He belched, and he was still burping when they were jolted and thrown sideways, crashing their heads against the wall of the container, a jumble of arms and legs, spilled beer, squashed pretzels.

Then silence. Fitz-Hume whistled, said a quick thanks to his Maker, and began undoing the clips. He was nearer the clasps. He undid them and pushed open the lid and instantly their senses were assaulted.

Later, thinking back on it, Millbarge reckoned that the smell was the most powerful he had ever experienced, a stench of rancid goats' milk and urine; next came the horrific sight of unwashed, bearded faces glaring at them as they clambered out.

Immediately it was obvious why they weren't being given a glad-hand welcome. They sniffed and looked down into a dungheap. Squashed mud and dung. They had landed on top of a mud hut.

"Oh shit," Millbarge muttered, searching the wreckage for bodies, but there were none.

The locals approached cautiously from the village. A hundred of them, maybe more, and all angry; fifty, maybe sixty ancient rifles pointing at them.

Fitz-Hume tweaked Millbarge's sleeve and whispered: "Toto, I don't think we're in Kansas anymore."

Millbarge scanned the crowd for a friendly face and found none. Weathered-skinned, confused-looking men and women wearing furs and boots and not one placard saying "Welcome."

"Is one of these guys our contact?" he asked.

"I'll check," said Fitz-Hume. He cupped his hands to his mouth and yelled: *"Who led the American League in home runs for 1953?"*

No response except for bolts being pulled back on rifles. Fitz-Hume thought fast, seeking sanctuary, then remembered the phrasebook given to him by some guy from the state department as they boarded the transport plane. Conversational Pashtu.

He pulled it from his tunic and hurriedly thumbed through the index.

General Difficulties. That was it. The two nastiest of the villagers had raised their rifles to their shoulders. Fitz-Hume grinned at them, held up one hand, asking for time, flipped through the booklet, and whooped silently to himself. The phrase he wanted leaped out of the page at him and he made himself a promise to take the author to the 21 Club for cocktails when he got home:

"If you permit me to go free, you may use my friend's head for polo."

He had no time to learn proper pronunciation and so he just roared out the translation, slowly and phonetically, and hoped for the best.

It worked. There was a roar of delight from the crowd. Rifles were lowered and the crowd swarmed around them, laughing and shouting, men and women scrambling over one another to feel Millbarge's head.

"What did you say?" Millbarge asked, reciprocating, stroking the nearest headgear that came to hand and smiling into faces full of broken teeth.

"I told them hello," said Fitz-Hume. "How are you? They're just saying hello."

Later maybe, he told himself, he could afford the luxury of guilt about Millbarge's head, but right now the only law was Darwin's: survival of the fittest.

His thoughts were interrupted by the sound of loud voices behind him, strident and authoritative. He turned and saw two white men pushing through the crowd. Clean-cut young men with blond college-boy haircuts and dressed like college freshmen, broad at the shoulder and narrow at the hip, shooing away the villagers as if they were geese.

Fitz-Hume was reminded of the Saturday-morning movies of his childhood, when he had wanted to look like Tab Hunter.

The first Tab Hunter reached them, smiled, showing a full set of even, sparkling teeth, and held out a tanned right hand.

"Hi, Bud Schnelker. Liaison Office. U.S. consulate, Karachi."

"Rob Hodges," said the other. "DIA. West Asian section. Welcome to Pakistan." Their handshakes were firm and dry. They exuded an odor of talcum powder and Old Spice.

Millbarge ducked out from beneath the huddle of villagers who were playing with his head and smiled. "You don't know how glad we are to see you guys," he said.

"Right," said Fitz-Hume. "When do we eat?"

Schnelker laughed heartily at Fitz-Hume's little joke and took his arm. "Come on, guys," he said. "The jeep's over here."

This was okay. This was confidence building, proof positive that even in the middle of nowhere old Uncle Sam looked after his own.

They had driven for half an hour and seen nothing, just mile after mile of dirt road through arid lifeless desert. Dry brown earth stretched to an unbroken blue horizon. Hodges drove with Schnelker next to him. Fitz-

Hume and Millbarge sat in the back, still burping from the early-morning beer.

They were starving and getting bored.

"So, where are we going?" Fitz-Hume yelled. "I mean, what's the deal here?"

Schnelker looked over his shoulder, no longer smiling. "You mean you guys don't know your final objective?"

"We don't know anything beyond this contact," Millbarge told him.

"Oh, that's too bad," said Schnelker, and turned his back on them.

Fitz-Hume tapped his shoulder. The man still hadn't answered his original question.

"Christ, I'm hungry," he said. "What time is it?"

Hodges leaned back, showing a watch.

"Nine o'clock," said Fitz-Hume. "I knew it. My stomach can always tell. Once I was—"

"Could we stop?" asked Millbarge urgently, interrupting him. He had stiffened and was looking uncomfortable.

"What's the matter?" Hodges asked.

"I gotta take a leak."

The jeep slowed and stopped. Hodges cut the engine and the silence battered their eardrums. There was nothing alive as far as they could see in all directions, no animal or plant, nowhere to seek any kind of privacy.

Millbarge thanked the driver, heaved himself out, leaned against the jeep, and looked hard at Fitz-Hume.

"You should go too," he said.

"What are you, my mother?" Fitz-Hume's tone was indignant. The two Tab Hunters were watching them carefully. "Don't you think I'm capable of determining my own time to go to the bathroom?"

Bathroom, thought Millbarge. An odd word out here. "So," he said patiently, "isn't this one of those times?"

"No."

Millbarge glanced at the others. They were staring at him. He couldn't even try a wink at Fitz-Hume; he just had to persevere.

"Come on," he coaxed. "You don't feel a certain degree of urgent pressure on the inner wall of your bladder? Now? Right at this moment?"

"No. I'm fine."

Christ, thought Millbarge. If this is the level of intelligence at the state department, the Free World's in big trouble.

He spoke slowly now, as if to a child.

"Wouldn't you really feel more comfortable being fully relieved of any excess fluids now? Immediately?"

Fitz-Hume's mouth opened in an *aaaah* of comprehension, reminding Millbarge of a fish on a slab.

"Okay, okay," Fitz-Hume said. "All right. What the hell." He jumped out and winked at the others. "Don't go away now," he said cheerfully.

"Oh, we won't."

They walked fast, close, as if embarrassed,

as if they were putting a lot of distance between themselves and the jeep so that the others wouldn't actually see them at it, hoping that Schnelker and Hodges wouldn't think it odd that two top men from Washington didn't like to be seen with their dicks out.

"These guys are not our legitimate contacts," said Millbarge out of the side of his mouth, an act made easier by their fifteen minutes in the centrifuge. "These guys are KGB Special Branch."

"Come on," said Fitz-Hume, ever the skeptic.

"Don't tell me to come on. That was a Russian wristwatch. I know the country of origin of every timepiece in the world. That was a Russian copy of a 1969 Timex digital."

Fitz-Hume was reluctantly impressed. "What? Your hobby or something? He stopped and Millbarge had to drag him along to make sure he didn't give himself away by looking back.

"Basic," Millbarge said. "It's one of the most common slipups in espionage. We've walked into enemy hands."

"I don't believe you," Fitz-Hume said.

"You better . . ." Then he stopped talking. Schnelker and Hodges were standing five or six paces in front of them. Millbarge had been so intent on convincing Fitz-Hume that he hadn't noticed them run around their flank. Now the two Russians were smiling at them, hands behind their backs like British royalty; fixed, friendly grins sparkling in the sun.

"Hi," said Fitz-Hume.

"Just between us," said Schnelker. "If you guys *do* know your final objective, you'd be smart to tell me. I could probably work things out a lot quicker for you."

Fitz-Hume finally accepted Millbarge's hypothesis. If these guys really were Tab Hunters, why would they be threatening them, even if the threat was delivered with a beachboy grin?

Then Millbarge began to have an idea. It wasn't original, almost as old as the gunman's trick of nodding to an absent someone behind his enemy so that he'd turn around. Almost as corny but worth a try.

"Yeah," he said. "You know what they say about this kind of operation. *Chepuha!*"

Schnelker nodded and smiled, said *"da, da,"* in agreement, then froze and groaned, slapped his forehead for his stupidity, then brought his gun from behind his back and aimed.

Fitz-Hume and Millbarge looked at each other. They had the idea simultaneously. It was pure luck, the fact that they were brought up in the same culture, on the same Saturday movies. They grinned, nodded, roared "FEET! HAT!" and snatched off their kepis, then jumped on the Russians' feet and jammed their hats on the two blond heads and pulled them over their eyes, turned, ran like Carl Lewis for the jeep, and threw themselves at it as the first bullet zipped past them. Fitz-Hume fumbled for the ignition, bucking the car away as Millbarge held on, feet dragging in the dust before clambering into the driver's seat, while the jeep zigzagged, taking fire in the rear end and the backseat, through the back doors.

And then they were out of range, Fitz-Hume whooping, kicking the accelerator, arms crossed on the wheel, fishtailing across the desert, while Millbarge pulled himself into a sitting position and looked back at the two tiny white figures, wondering what they were thinking.

This meant Siberia for them. It was the salt mines or the psychiatric hospitals.

Served them right, and in that moment he knew why America and the Free World would always have an edge over the Soviets. It was culture. The Soviets didn't have Hope and Crosby. They didn't know how to cope in a crisis.

—Twelve—

It took them awhile to get their breath back, realize what they had done and where they were, and ponder the possibility that they were actually beginning to enjoy themselves. This was something to tell the Alices and the Jennifers and anyone else who cared to listen.

This adventure could get them laid.

"Boy," said Fitz-Hume. "What a burn. They sure fooled me. We should avoid those guys for the rest of our lives." He sneaked a glance at Millbarge. The big buy wasn't so dumb after all. His head was for more than being kicked around at polo. Fitz-Hume felt an unfamiliar twinge of guilt. He felt he owed Millbarge one.

"Where to, boss?" he said, placing himself

in the subservient role, happy to let Millbarge
make the decisions.

Millbarge shrugged.

"What do we do now besides drive fast and
far?" Fitz-Hume persisted.

"Well, the first thing we should do is for-
mulate a plan."

"To get us to the nearest airport."

Millbarge nodded.

"So what's the plan?"

"First, we have to take stock of our gaso-
line supplies." He turned and began counting. "Ten cans, five gallons apiece. Land
rovers get around eleven to the gallon. Figure four hundred and fifty miles."

"That'll get us to the nearest airport," said
Fitz-Hume happily.

"Okay," said Millbarge. "We do it in shifts.
One drives while the other sleeps."

"Okay. You sleep."

"Good. Okay. Great. Wake me up when
you get tired." He slumped into his seat with
a goodnight.

"Goodnight," said Fitz-Hume, winking at
him, feeling friendly. "Sleep tight."

Millbarge opened one eye.

"Don't let the bedbugs bite."

Millbarge slumped further. Within minutes he was snoring.

Fitz-Hume drove for hours and saw nothing. Now and again the monotony was relieved when the road dipped and ran along-

side a ravine, but mostly it was just desert and sun. Fitz-Hume yawned, wishing he had a radio or a tape deck, and idly wondered what was so great about Pakistan or Afghanistan. If Afghanistan was like this, why would the Russians want it? He didn't know. If truth be known, politics baffled him, but he didn't care. You didn't need politics to be a diplomat.

By noon he was shivering, the high sun casting no shadows. Sunstroke was coming on. He'd had it once before when he'd taken that little Jewish princess to Miami. But this was worse. They shouldn't have lost their hats.

He was beginning to worry now. He'd never been exactly adventurous, always took foreign holidays somewhere safe, prepaid, through a Washington travel firm, wouldn't go anywhere outside an hour's drive from an Amex office. He liked to know where the facilities were, like the nearest American doctor.

This was far too remote for his taste. He worried. What if they blew a tire and crashed? What if he got appendicitis? This kind of place wouldn't recognize Blue Cross. You could cut yourself shaving and bleed to death out here and no one would know for a year.

Plus he was beginning to hallucinate, thought he saw Omar Sharif in his Laurence of Arabia outfit on the horizon.

He slowed as he drew near. The horizon gradually stopped shimmering and he could make out a man on a camel.

Black robes, a black headband and a rifle. Fitz-Hume stopped a few yards from him and the man looked impassively at him; he was the stuff of desert musicals: hawk-nosed, dark-eyed, a scarf covering his mouth.

"Good morning," Fitz-Hume said. "Could you direct us to the nearest airport?"

In reply the man raised his rifle, turned to the horizon, and bawled something incomprehensible. Fitz-Hume looked to see what Millbarge made of it. Millbarge snored back at him, happily oblivious.

When he looked back, the horizon was beaded with movement. He shaded his eyes and saw dozens of men on horseback, maybe hundreds. A dust storm answering the camel man's yell.

Fitz-Hume nudged Millbarge awake with an elbow and an urgent message: "Your turn to drive."

Millbarge awakened as the first horsemen arrived and clattered to a halt. A moment later they were clustering around the jeep; fierce men with guns and swords, lean and hungry men, Fitz-Hume thought. They made the last lot look harmless.

"Hey," Millbarge whispered. "These are the Yusufzais, Afghan freedom fighters. They're our allies."

Fitz-Hume grinned with relief and stood

up, one hand on the wheel, the other waving, his hi-there-guys smile on full beam.

"We're Americans," he shouted.

The Yusufzais growled. Maybe, Millbarge thought, something got lost in the translation.

— *Thirteen* —

For half an hour they had been hanging
upside-down, their ankles lashed to a cross-
beam supported by bamboo poles. Their hands
were tied behind them. Their hair brushed
the dirt.

Side by side they turned and swiveled.
They could see tents and flimsy huts and
Yusufzai warriors moving restlessly among
them. They were heavily armed. Fitz-Hume
reckoned they wouldn't look out of place in
the South Bronx. Evil-looking bastards in
fur jackets, leggings, and boots, most of them
scarred or maimed in one way or another.

Millbarge had to keep reminding himself
that these people were his friends. Rhombus
had said so. Your enemy's enemy is your
friend, he had told them, but right now, it
wasn't a convincing argument, and besides,

the blood had gone to their heads; there was no feeling in their legs; another few minutes of this and it would be goodnight.

Upside-down youths with rifles gaped at them.

An ancient, upside-down warrior kept running his thumb along a rusty knife and taking practice swipes at them. He was one-eyed and toothless—the village idiot maybe—but he could flash his knife okay. They could feel the slipstream as it zipped around their throats.

This wasn't so good. But Fitz-Hume had a plan. He was about to whisper it when two shadows fell across them. One was English with a BBC accent and talking to the other shadow.

"What *do* you think you're doing, Chief?" A supercilious drawl of superior breeding, as confident as if there were still a British empire. "Tell your man to cut them down."

A grunt of instruction and the old man's face was a picture of disappointment. With two strokes he cut them free and they crumpled into the dust, then scrambled on dead legs into a crouch and looked up into two strange faces.

The chief was enormous. A heavy black beard, matted hair, hook nose, and black angry eyes. He wore tattered furs and goatskin boots and looked down at them as if they had just crawled from beneath a rock.

The Englishman was slim, wearing a cap

at an angle and a safari suit. He could have stepped out of a Noel Coward comedy. All that was missing was the cigarette holder. He was smiling.

"Sorry about this," he drawled. "They're very distrustful of outsiders. They only allow us here because we're helping with the wounded."

They struggled to their feet, holding on to his arms for support, thanking him and asking who he was, the blood draining back into their legs.

"Oh, sorry. Hadley," he said, shaking hands. "London College of Medicine. They didn't realize you were with the effort."

"With what?" Fitz-Hume asked.

"Why, the United Nations Medical Effort, of course." He blinked at them expectantly. Fitz-Hume and Millbarge hopped around him in embarrassed ignorance. Their feet were still bound by rope.

"Aren't you Doctors Trowbridge and Greenberg?"

Then the chief butted in, poking them suspiciously: "You doctors?"

That settled it. "Yeah, yeah . . ." they said together.

"Trowbridge," said Fitz-Hume, trying to remember, "and . . . uh . . ."

"Greenbaum," said Millbarge.

"Berg," said Fitz-Hume, remembering now.

"Berg," parroted Millbarge. "Greenbaumberg."

"Berg," said Fitz-Hume again.

"We're doctors," said Millbarge.

The chief didn't look convinced. Millbarge reckoned they needed proof. He grinned and looked around him. "Well, everybody here looks okay." Then he turned to the chief. "Stick out your tongue."

The chief did as he was asked. Everyone does what a doctor tells them, Millbarge thought. The tongue looked like a street map of Hoboken. Fitz-Hume patted it.

"Yeah. Everybody's fine. We'll be heading back to the old UN now, tell them what a good job you're doing."

Hadley smiled and took his arm. "Ah, the American sense of humor. Come on, the others are anxious to meet you."

There was nothing for it. He hopped along with Hadley, Fitz-Hume behind, hopping alongside the chief, through the villa campsite to the largest of the tents, a small UN flag fluttering from the flagpole.

Inside, the doctors had assembled. There were six of them but Fitz-Hume could see only one. She was tall, blond, blue-eyed, slim, with cheekbones made in heaven and smiling at him. Cross Lauren Hutton with Bo Derek and you've almost got her.

Millbarge sniffed, the smell of morphine, a hospital smell, looked around at the cases of drugs and bandages, then at the group of doctors, identically dressed in brown safari suits, and tried to pay attention as Hadley made the introductions.

"Well, here we are," he said cheerfully. "I'm Hadley, internal medicine." He pointed to a small Oriental woman. "Dr. La Fong, communicable diseases." Then to each of the others. "Dr. Boyer, bacteriology . . ."

Fitz-Hume smiled. This was the one. Boyer. He tried to think of a rhyme for it, something rude he could say on their pillow . . .

"Doctors Stinson, Marston, and Gill from Northampton Trauma Institute. And Dr. Imhaus of the Zurich Relief Fund."

Hadley nodded toward Fitz-Hume and Millbarge. "These," he announced, "are our newly arrived surgeons, Doctors Trowbridge and Greenbaum."

Dr. La Fong made a small bow to Millbarge. "Doctor," she said.

"Doctor," replied Millbarge.

"Doctor," she said, bowing to Fitz-Hume.

"Doctor," said Fitz-Hume.

"Doctor," said Boyer.

"Doctor," said Millbarge.

"Doctor," said Boyer.

"Doctor," said Millbarge.

"Doctor," said Imhaus.

"Doctor," said Millbarge.

"Doctor," said Stinson.

"Doctor," said Fitz-Hume.

"Doctor," said Marston.

"Doctor," said Millbarge.

"Doctor," said Gill.

"Doctor," said Boyer again.

"Doctor," said Fitz-Hume.

A pause.

"We miss anyone?" Millbarge asked.

They hadn't. Hadley rubbed his hands and beamed at them.

"Now why don't you gentlemen relax," he said. "The tribe is planning a raid against a Soviet tank battalion tomorrow. You'll have plenty to do then."

"Fine. We'll do that," said Millbarge.

Hadley nodded and began shepherding the doctors out, then held out his hand. "Doctor," he said to Millbarge.

"Doctor," said Millbarge.

Hadley went out, followed by La Fong. She "doctored" both of them and they "doctored" her back. Then Imhaus, Stinson, Marston, and Gill.

Boyer was the last to leave. Fitz-Hume did not shake her hand. He kissed it. Her fingers fluttered against his throat; a promise of ecstasy.

Then she was gone and Millbarge was shaking him, saying they had to get out of this place immediately. Fitz-Hume shook his head. He wasn't leaving, not till he'd gotten to know Dr. Boyer a whole lot better. Millbarge grabbed him by the shoulders and tried to shake some sense into him but Fitz-Hume was glassy-eyed, gazing over his shoulder at something. Millbarge turned and saw Boyer looking in.

"Excuse me," she said. "Am I interrupting?"

"No," Fitz-Hume said, shoving Millbarge toward the flap. "He was just leaving."

Boyer stepped nimbly inside as Millbarge was hurled out, protesting, tripping over a guy rope and falling heavily.

Fitz-Hume smiled. "Hi," he said.

"Dr. Trowbridge," said Boyer.

"Where?" asked Fitz-Hume, momentarily confused. Then he remembered. Lust played havoc with his memory. Always had. "Oh yes. What can I do for you?"

"Dr. Trowbridge ... may I call you Homer?"

"Why?"

"That's your name."

Fitz-Hume laughed to hide his embarrassment and his rotten memory. "Yes, of course. Homer. What's your name?"

"Karen." She smiled and he thought he saw the hint of a blush on the perfect cheeks. Briefly she lowered her eyes as if embarrassed, then took a deep breath. His gaze shifted, then moved back up again to her face as she grasped his hand. "Dr. Trowbridge, Homer, when you walked in this hut, it was the most exciting moment of my life."

"Just wait," he said, looking at her leeringly.

"You're a hero of mine," she said. "I've read all your papers."

"How did you get my papers?" he stuttered, then realized what she was talking about. Think medicine, he told himself. "Oh, papers. You mean medical papers. Right?"

"Are you making fun of me?" she said, stepping back.

"Oh, Karen. Our first fight."

She smiled. This was good. She liked his jokes. He asked her to sit and watched, hungrily, as she took off her jacket and sat on a bench. She was wearing a white T-shirt. Fitz-Hume had never seen such a T-shirt, and what made it better was the things she was saying.

"You might think I'm silly to worship you the way I do, but in my estimation you're a genius."

This called for modesty. "*Genius* is a strong word," he said. "However, if you insist, I can handle it."

She looked away from him. "In fact I hesitate to mention my problem. It's a task hardly worthy of your abilities."

He was by her side in a bound, stroking her hands. "What? Problem? Go ahead. Mention it. There's nothing I wouldn't do for you."

"It's the Khan's brother."

Khan, he thought? Must be the big guy, the chief.

"He's been suffering from pain in the right-lower abdomen," she continued. "Obviously an inflamed appendix."

"Obviously."

"Dr. Hadley was going to remove it but

now that you're here . . . I mean, just to see you perform even this simple piece of surgery would be one of the great thrills of my life."

This was a problem. Reluctantly he pulled away from her, got to his feet, and began pacing. "I . . . uh . . . it's . . . I'd rather not. I don't have any instruments. I dropped them in quicksand."

She was quickly behind him, turning him to face her, beseeching him. "You can use Dr. Hadley's. Please, Homer. The Khan's brother is being prepped right now. If you refuse to do it, the Khan will lose faith in you . . . in us. The consequences could be severe."

"I see," he said, thinking on his feet. "Well, the truth is, I am a great surgeon, but alas, I've recently suffered severe damage in my left hand."

"Oh, my God." Her hands fluttered to her lips, leaving her breasts unguarded. Fitz-Hume continued thinking.

"No feeling at all," he said, flapping his hand around like a drag queen, then letting it fall on to her right breast. "See that?" he said. "Nothing. Dead."

He had told some lies in his time—little white ones, big black ones—but this was a whopper.

She believed him, didn't slap his face, didn't even move a muscle.

"How did . . . ?" she whimpered, but he interrupted her.

"I was lifting a car off a child," he improvised. "Big car. Cadillac."

Boyer shook her head. "I'm so let down. And the Khan. He'll be very suspicious. My God."

"There, there," he said, patting the other breast with his good hand and leaving it there. Still she did not move. Then he had another brainstorm. "I can perform surgery without my hands."

Her eyes widened as he continued. "Dr. Greenbaum. He's my hands now. I tell him what to do and he does it. So you will get to see me in action."

A brief tremor of guilt ran through him but he ignored it, concentrating on Boyer, who was saying, "Wonderful." The only problem was that she had pulled his hands away and was holding them by his sides.

"Of course," he said wistfully, "after I guide Dr. Greenbaum through an operation, I'm very depressed that I couldn't do it myself. That's a very bad time for me."

She looked up at him with what he hoped was adoration. "I'll be with you," she whispered.

It was time. The moment had come. He kissed her. She squirmed. He put his arms around her. She pushed herself hard against him. The flap opened and Millbarge walked in.

"Gimme a break," Fitz-Hume groaned.

They broke apart and she moved away. "About one hour?" she said.

"Oh, I can go much longer than that," he said, then understood. "Ah, until the operation." He flopped his useless hand in farewell and she left, blowing him a kiss.

Millbarge looked at him and shook his head in disgust, but Fitz-Hume was on fire. He grabbed Millbarge's hands and leered at him.

"Hey, you're good with tools, aren't you? Instruments? Devices?"

Millbarge pulled away and held up his hands like Al Jolson.

"What? Are you kidding?" he said. "You're talking to Millbarge. You want it built, repaired, modified, converted, or dismantled, you're talking to Mr. Hands."

Fitz-Hume grinned. The man had just committed himself. He was about to explain when something tinkled behind them. They twitched, startled, and turned. A golf ball had bounced off a clay jug. A moment later Bob Hope appeared through the flap, smiling at them and carrying a golf club. At least, the man looked like Bob Hope, the very image of him, and when he spoke, he sounded just like him.

"Mind if I play through?"

They nodded dumbly.

The man who looked like Bob Hope took a stance behind the ball, made a neat little swing with what looked like a five iron, and the ball was chipped through the flap—a perfect shot.

The Bob Hope figure followed it, stopped for a moment, grinned, and said: "Doctor," to Millbarge, "Doctor," to Fitz-Hume. "I'm glad I'm not sick."

Then he was gone.

They closed their eyes, thinking identically: it was the heat. A mirage. Fitz-Hume vowed never to tell Millbarge what he thought he had just seen. The man would think he was going crazy.

And Millbarge made precisely the same vow.

— *Fourteen* —

An hour later Millbarge was still raging, wondering how he had let himself be talked into this ludicrous, dangerous situation. He ranted and raved, he stamped his foot, but Fitz-Hume only laughed. Millbarge's problem was that they were both wearing green surgical gowns and skullcaps—no one could take an angry man seriously when he was dressed that way.

Still, Millbarge persisted. He had been roaring so long that he was getting hoarse.

"This is impossible. This is nuts. This is surgery." He slapped a thick medical book on the boards that had been set up as the operating table and swore long and loud.

" 'This is surgery,' " Fitz-Hume said, mimicking him. "Okay, fine. Don't do it. You wanna end up like this?"

He picked up a mummified human head wrapped in rags and tied with leather thongs.

"Where did you get that?" Millbarge wanted to know.

"Polo field. And this isn't the only part they play with," he said nastily. "Get the picture?"

Millbarge did. There was no escape. And all this, he thought, for the hundredth time, for cheating on an exam.

The flap parted and a man was carried in on a pallet by four bare-chested bearers and gently laid on the table. Millbarge hurriedly threw the medical book underneath as the doctors filed in and grouped themselves around him. They all wore surgical gowns and stood with hands clasped in front of them; like mourners, Millbarge thought.

The flap opened again and the Khan strode in, followed by a group of his men. He surveyed the scene and nodded.

"If anything happens to him," he said, pointing to his brother, "my people will be angry. To die in battle is glorious. To die in a hut is a disgrace."

A murmur of assent rumbled round the tent. Fitz-Hume silenced it by holding up one hand.

"And with that, I give you Dr. Julius Greenberg." He pushed Greenbaum forward. "Doctor," he said.

"Thank you, Doctor," said Millbarge.

"I'll be outside having a smoke," said Fitz-

Dan Aykroyd as
Austin Millbarge

Chevy Chase as
Emmett Fitz-Hume

Donna Dixon as
Karen Boyer

Spies Like Us

On its thirty-eighth day in orbit Nasa Satellite, Hi-Weather IV, spots something . . . Sixty feet of steel cylinder, a large red star on its hull.

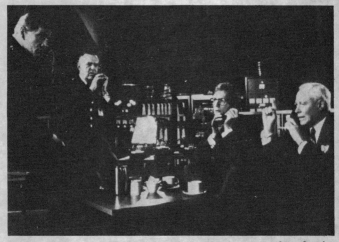

. . . A cause for some alarm for the powers that be in Washington.

Millbarge (*above*) watches, fascinated, as Fitz-Hume (*below*) goes through his routine of prying his eye-patch off, reading something on the inside and writing it down.

"This is your standard bog-negotiation trial."

This will verify your ability to stay afloat at high speeds, you will have ropes tied to your wrists.

"If you permit me to go free, you may use my friend's head for polo."

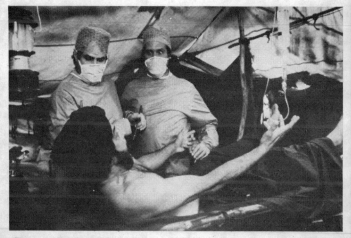

"Doctor, isn't that incision a little high for the appendix?"

Millbarge and Fitz-Hume perched upon their only mode of transportation head for the Pamir District.

"Something stopped him, something furry and warm and sticky. Bodies, each one staining the snow with blood."

Dressed as aliens from outerspace they descend upon the Russian soldiers' campsite.

It took exactly eight seconds. A low rumble of ignition turned into a roar, smoke belched from the base of the rocket, and then the first flames. "I think we just started World War III," says Millbarge softly.

"It'll take about twenty-eight minutes before that rocket hits its target inside the continental United States. I figure we have about forty-two minutes until the end of civilization as we know it."

Hume, heading for the door as Millbarge pulled him back, angrily. "Or perhaps I'll stay," he said, bowing to the inevitable.

Millbarge surveyed the spectators and rubbed his hands. The rubber squeaked.

"Um ... today we'll be removing the patient's appendix. The first thing to do is ..." And with that he dived under the table and vanished, thumbed down the page, popped back up, smiled: "... shave the patient."

The Khan's brother was slimmer than the Khan, but even unconscious, he managed to look menacing. He was dressed only in a loincloth, his features obscured by a thick beard.

Millbarge felt the thickness of the beard and held up a shaving brush. Fitz-Hume slapped his hand away and smiled apologetically at the watching doctors. They didn't smile back, and Fitz-Hume felt like the straight man in a dying vaudeville act.

"Well, let's skip the shave," Millbarge was saying, "and go right to the operation. Next we need ..." He dived again for the book, came up again like a drowning man and announced: "... the anaesthetic."

A thin voice questioned, concerned. It was La Fong. "But can't you tell? He's already been given the required injection of pentathol."

"Ah, of course," Millbarge said. "And now for the incision."

He fumbled in the tray, closed his eyes,

and took pot luck, came up with a sharp
object and showed it around, like a magician
with a wand, then placed it on the patient's
chest.

"Doctor," shouted Imhaus urgently. "Isn't
that incision just a little high for the appendix?"

Now Millbarge's anger flooded to the surface. His cheeks went pink. He stamped his
foot again. "You wanna do it?" he yelled.
"You wanna do the operation? Fine. Come
on up and you do it."

Hadley tutted and admonished Imhaus,
shushed him up, but the man wouldn't be
pacified.

"He was cutting into his chest," he protested.

"Did you see me cut his chest?" Millbarge
roared. "Did I cut his chest?" He looked from
face to face, then lowered his voice and talked
gently to them, like a lecturer to his stu-
dents. "I was probing to determine muscle
tone and skeletal girth. It's a new technique."
He waggled his scalpel in the direction of his
tormentor. "We mock what we don't understand."

"Yeah," broke in Fitz-Hume, patting Millbarge on the back. "Go ahead. I'm hungry."

"Okay. The first incision."

He placed the scalpel against the patient's
stomach, his thumb on the blunt edge like
he'd seen in "Marcus Welby," and glanced

up at the doctors. They were shaking their heads.

He moved it lower, looked up. They still didn't approve. Another couple of inches. They nodded.

"Yes," said Fitz-Hume, who had been testing the reactions. "That's it, Doctor."

"Thank you. I will now make the incision."

He hesitated. This was no time to tell Fitz-Hume that he always fainted at the sight of blood. Fitz-Hume took a last look at the audience. Above her surgical mask, Boyer winked at him. He waved a floppy hand at her, then turned back to the job and whispered: "Go ahead. Cut the sucker."

Millbarge closed his eyes and pressed. The patient sat up fast, eyes popping open, tongue distended, arms held out as if in prayer, then he gurgled, a low, rasping moan, and collapsed. Prone. Going blue.

Imhaus was first to his side, taking his pulse. He knew a heart attack when he saw one.

"This man is dead," he announced.

Commotion among the doctors. The Khan seemed not to understand. Fitz-Hume and Millbarge did not wait for the translation. Slowly but purposefully they strode out of the tent, stopped briefly at the flap, then walked fast down the hill, whistling cheerfully as if nothing awful had happened, as if no disgrace had befallen the Khan's brother, as if there was absolutely no chance of their heads being used in a polo match.

An old ambulance was parked a hundred yards away, at the edge of the camp. Millbarge nudged Fitz-Hume, pointed to it, jangled the ignition keys in his pocket, and winked.

While Fitz-Hume had been flirting with Boyer, Austin Millbarge had been planning a retreat.

They ran. Behind them came a bellow of rage. The Afghans by their tents blinked up at them drowsily. Luck was in. It was siesta time.

Fifty yards to go and the first bullet whined past their ears. Stumbling, gasping, breaking all sprint records, hurdling a youth who tried to tackle them, they made it to the ambulance, Millbarge yanking the door open and throwing out a sleeping Afghan as if he were a sack of laundry. He clambered into the driver's seat, Fitz-Hume behind him, and said a short prayer.

It was answered. The engine started on the first turn. He kicked in the clutch, stamped on the accelerator, and the old machine bucked away, heading north. In the side mirror Fitz-Hume could see the Afghans leaping on horses and he briefly closed his eyes and crossed his fingers.

Ambulances were built for speed, weren't they? They had to be fast to go at life-or-death speed.

But could it beat a horse? That was the question.

He did a brave thing, stuck his head out of the window, and didn't like what he saw. The Afghans were gaining, fifty of them at a rough guess and all with rifles. It was a scene out of *Stagecoach*. He slumped back in his seat, petrified, as the first bullets smacked into the chassis and he tried not to think of polo. He had been to a match once, in Palm Beach. They hit the ball very hard.

A thump and he looked in the mirror again. The leading Afghan had tried a stunt, thrown himself at the back door, missed, and now he was being trampled by the others and shaking his fist.

One down, thought Fitz-Hume. Forty-nine to go.

Bullets riddled the ambulance. Automatic fire. Probably, U.S.-issued weapons, thought Millbarge. There was something indecent about being shot at by your own country's weapons. The steering wheel bucked and jerked in his hands like a live thing and he fought for control, briefly wondering why the Afghans didn't shoot out the tires. Maybe up here they hadn't heard about rubber. Maybe they didn't know about flat tires. Maybe they hadn't discovered the goddamn wheel yet.

Concentrating hard, tongue clamped between his teeth, he didn't see the warrior a couple of feet away, a big man, one hand loose on the reins, the other thrusting his rifle through the open window. Millbarge felt something tickle his ear. A fly, he

thought. He brushed it away, felt something
cold and metallic, and looked into the barrel
of a gun at a brown fist, a brown finger on
the trigger, squeezing.

He shrieked and backhanded the rifle away
from him, took both hands off the wheel, and
rolled up the window, fast, the rider dropping back, off balance, the rifle dangling im-
potently from Millbarge's window.

But now there were Afghans to the right
of them, Afghans to the left of them, and an
Afghan on the roof. Instinctively he and Fitz-
Hume looked up as a burst of automatic fire
blasted holes in the cabin and shattered the
windscreen.

Fitz-Hume began to shake uncontrollably
but Millbarge only laughed, the chuckle of a
maniac. He had seen something ahead. It
was Saturday matinee time again. A clump
of trees. Laughing hysterically, he drove
toward them.

A thump and the Afghan was gone. Millbarge sneaked a glance in his mirror and
saw him, hanging on to the branch that had
knocked him off and waving his fist.

The culture again. They didn't have the
culture.

He was still laughing when he smelled
rancid goats' milk and felt bony hands on
his neck, throttling him. He lost control of
the wheel as he struggled. The ambulance
skidded and banged into a horse, throwing
an Afghan into the dirt.

Nice trick, Fitz-Hume thought, looking back in his mirror, wondering why Millbarge hadn't thought of it sooner. Then he was aware of a gurgling sound. He turned to see a furry figure battling with Millbarge and instinctively his innate cowardice asserted itself.

"Austin," he wheezed. "There's someone choking you."

It was the first time he had used Millbarge's Christian name.

"Help," Millbarge croaked.

The ambulance lurched and threw Fitz-Hume hard against the little man in furs. He was young and lithe but no match for two men in the grip of terror.

They grabbed fur and threw him out, fast. He didn't even bounce, just flew straight out the back of the ambulance and bowled over the nearest horse.

Millbarge grabbed the wheel again and pushed hard against the accelerator. Into the floor. The speedo dancing.

And suddenly they were on their own. The sound of gunfire was receding. Fitz-Hume took a chance and leaned out. The Afghans were falling back. Their horses had run out of steam.

Technology, thought Fitz-Hume. You couldn't beat it.

—Fifteen—

Halfway around the world and across the time zones, a station wagon bearing U.S. government plates was traveling across the desert parallel to the runaway ambulance.

But this was American desert. It had roads, gas stations, drive-in movies. This was Nevada at dusk.

Ruby was driving and he was uncomfortable. The air conditioning couldn't cope with the heat and Ruby was a man accustomed to a constant manufactured temperature. His life had been lived at sixty-eight degrees. Anything higher or lower disturbed his equilibrium. Deserts he could do without.

Next to him, Keyes was equally uncomfortable and discomfort made him irritable. He was studying a map and making little sense of it.

"All the funds they're pouring into this project," he grumbled. "You'd think they could have at least sent someone to pick us up."

"I suppose so," said Ruby. "But I doubt they can spare any personnel with the go-hour less than forty-eight hours away."

Keyes grunted, threw the map away, looked up, and spotted their destination.

"There it is." He pointed. They'd made it.

As they approached the drive-in theater, Ruby whistled softly. It was an incongruous sight in the middle of nowhere, a weird kind of oasis. Ruby wondered what type of audience it must have attracted when it had been functioning. People must have driven for hours. The nearest town was Reno and that was God-knows-how-many miles away.

They stopped at the gate. A sign said:

LANCASTER DRIVE-IN NUMBER 3

The paint on the marquee had peeled and faded in the sun. Once it must have been bright azure and red. Now it had faded to a washed-out pink and pale blue. The screen still stood facing south and Keyes' imagination did a backflip, flashing memories of his youth—of feverish evenings with girls from high school and the odd glimpse of Gable and Company over their shoulders.

Ruby was about to get out when two men appeared from the gatehouse. They were

young, wearing denims, with a lot of muscle
that was fairly irrelevant since they both
carried pump-action shotguns. They stood by
the gate, unsmiling, the older one cocking
his head at the notice.

"The drive-in is closed," he said, stating
the obvious in a tone of voice that said
get-the-hell-outta-here.

Keyes opened his window, smiled at them,
and said: "We're from the Ace Tomato Company."

The guards nodded, lifted a barrier, and
stood back. Ruby and Keyes got out of the
car, tossed the younger guard the keys, and
went through.

"Jesus," said Ruby. "Look at this place."

Weeds had strangled the posts that once
held the speakers. Ancient popcorn boxes and
beer cans crackled under their feet. The pink-
and-blue blockhouse that once held the projector was a crumbling ruin, the café a peel-
ing hovel. Keyes tried to imagine what the
last picture show must have been; probably
something with Hedy Lamarr in it.

"All this cloak-and-dagger stuff," he mumbled. "The military loves it."

They picked their way toward the café,
and Ruby felt nervous, worrying about his
shoes. He was out of his element in this
place, walking on broken earth. Anything
that hadn't been concreted over, he reckoned, was suspect. Then Keyes said something that added to his nervousness.

"Watch for snakes."

"Christ," he said, then stopped in his tracks as three men appeared from the café. Big men, two white, one black, and staring at them.

"Mr. Ruby," said one.

"Mr. Keyes," said another.

They nodded.

The third pointed to the café door. "Why don't you gentlemen have a Pepsi?" he said.

Briefly Ruby was about to tell the guy that he drank only Tab, but the look on the faces stopped him. Pepsi was an acquired taste and it looked like he was going to have to acquire it fast.

They smiled and made their way into the café as one of the guards spoke into the radio.

"Two Pepsis to go," he said.

The place was a litter bin of paper coffee cups and soft-drink bottles. They surveyed it for a moment and then moved between the tables to the counter. They walked behind it, trailing their fingers in the desert dust, then around again to the front.

"Now what?" asked Ruby.

"Have a Pepsi," said Keyes, pointing to a line of taps.

Ruby shrugged, drew a paper cup from the dispenser, placed it under the tap, and pressed the Pepsi button.

The earth moved.

The linoleum zipped away from under their feet and they found themselves standing on an iron grating. With a whirr of machinery, a cage of aluminium thrust itself out of the floor and trapped them. They had no time to wonder what was happening. A click, then the cage dropped fast, so fast that their stomachs lurched and their ears popped. Their hair stood on end.

They opened their mouths to yell but no sound came. All they could see was a concrete shaft and they could feel the updraft of cool air from deep underground.

They dropped, it seemed, for an eternity, then the cage slowed and came to a gentle stop. The concrete shaft had become a steel door, inches from their faces. A gentle whirr and it opened, and they stepped hesitantly out into a corridor painted military green, lit with neon. Two military police stood in front of them, guns on hips.

"This way, gentlemen," said one, then led the way, the other taking the rear.

Keyes touched the wall as he walked toward a glass door. It was metallic and cold. He shivered, then they were through the doors and being saluted by two well-known faces, neon glinting off their campaign medals.

"Welcome to WAMP," said General Sline.

"What?" said Ruby.

"The newest in transportable World Activity Monitoring Positions," said Miegs proudly. "WAMP."

"Oh," said Keyes, as Sline took his arm and led him along another corridor, with Miegs and Ruby following.

"It's Zulu-6000," Sline said. "We're getting ready here on our end. Where are your GLG-20s?"

"The main team is on schedule, and in their last satellite communication they informed us they are proceeding unimpeded to the strike zone."

"And your decoys?" he asked.

It was Ruby who answered. "By now I think we can assume they have been intercepted by enemy contacts," he said smugly.

"How can you be sure?" Miegs asked.

Keyes smiled at him. "Because we leaked their arrival to the KGB in Karachi."

They had reached a door marked "Command Bridge." It was guarded by two military policemen with automatic pistols in their hands—cocked, ready to fire. They stood to the side as Sline pushed the door open.

Ruby whistled in appreciation. The place was small, fifteen feet across, a pentagon shape. Seven technicians in blue uniforms sat at computer banks. Above them, monitors flashed pictures and data. There were three shots of satellites in orbit and color stills of a section of snow-covered forest.

Multicolored lights flashed from every square foot of equipment. Tapes of data chattering from the slits of receivers were automatically snipped off and sent by conveyer belt to the monitors.

Such a place, thought Ruby. It looked as though it could take you to Mars.

At the sound of the door opening, one of the technicians turned. He was holding a telephone and saluting.

"General Sline, sir."

"Yes, Sergeant."

"It's a collect call from Pakistan for Mr. Ruby. A Mr. Fitz-Hume."

A silence exploded through the room, then Ruby yelled: "What? Are you sure? How did he reach me here?"

The technician shrugged a "don't know" at him. "It's person-to-person, sir. Collect. They said their contacts tried to kill them and they don't know what they're supposed to do."

"And they told this to you?" said Keyes, astounded, his composure, for once, in tatters. "Over a public phone?"

"No, sir. The A. T. and T. operator told our operator."

"They're insane," Keyes whispered.

"And apparently roaming free," said Ruby, suddenly feeling very cold. This was dreadful. If this got out, his career was in jeopardy. This was a front page in the *Washington Post*. This was Dan Rather on the evening news. Already, instinctively, Ruby was working on his official denial.

"He's on the line, sir," said the technician.

Ruby grabbed the receiver from him and spat a hello down the line. "Fitz-Hume," he snapped, "where are you?"

Fitz-Hume was hopping mad. The phone, nailed to a post outside the Gilgit-Bunji bus depot, was the only one in a hundred miles. It had taken three hours for their call to get through and they'd had to fight off the natives to get to the phone when the connection was finally made.

Now a line of them stood muttering behind them. According to the state-department paper, the Pakistanis were an easygoing bunch with a *mañana* philosophy, but this lot were showing signs of starting a battle. And besides, he'd been bitten on the ankle by a rooster.

He was in no mood to suffer the anger of a jerk like Ruby.

"Where am I?" he roared. "I'm in the Third World. Get us out of here."

Millbarge grabbed the phone and barked at him: "This is not proper department procedure. This could destroy the entire mission."

Fitz-Hume gave him the finger. "Here's your mission." Then he leaned into the phone and bawled: "Guess what? We quit."

Millbarge turned away from him and tried for reason, fighting to repair the damage.

"This is Millbarge," he said sweetly. "I'm sorry about the break in policy but our contacts tried to kill us. We need to know the next step. . . ."

Then Fitz-Hume had wrestled the phone from him and was roaring again: "GET US OUT OF HERE!"

In the WAMP bunker, Ruby, for the first time in his professional life, was having trouble remaining calm.

"Everything's under control, Mr. Fitz-Hume." He noticed Keyes gesturing to him. "Hold on one moment," he said, and cupped the phone.

"Look," Keyes said. "The longer we keep them out in the field, the more heat they can draw away from the real team."

Ruby nodded. The man was right. He was a true legend, turning disadvantage into advantage, supremely cool under pressure. An admirable man.

"I agree," Sline was saying. "Let's send them over the border."

"How will they get there?" Keyes asked.

"That's their problem," Ruby said, seizing the initiative once more. He turned back to the phone and fixed a smile and a reassuring tone. "Gentlemen, hello. We are arranging a rescue operation for you."

Keyes leaned over and spoke into the receiver. "For *after* you've reached your final objective."

Fitz-Humes' angry voice crackled into the room. "What is our final objective?"

"Information like that is given out on a

need-to-know basis only," said Ruby, "and at this time you do not need to know. However, we can tell you to make immediately for the Soviet Pamir district."

"Where's that?" Fitz-Hume crackled.

"Wait for your next contact on the road to Dushanbe."

And he hung up, still smiling, a crisis averted. But Sline and Miegs weren't smiling. They were looking angry. If this were Washington, it would be easy. They could be fed a soothing drink. They could get laid. But this was a military bunker in the middle of nowhere. Suddenly Ruby felt vulnerable. Outmaneuvered and a little scared.

"The road to Dushanbe," Miegs said nastily, "You practically told them the strike zone."

Ruby shrugged and grinned as if he didn't have a care in the world. "Listen," he said. "Even if they get there at all, they'll be plucked by Soviet motorized infantry. The road to Dushanbe is a heavily traveled military artery."

The generals didn't look convinced but Keyes was happy. "I guess that takes care of that," he said, and rubbed his hands.

But Slime was not so sure. "There can be no mistake this time, gentlemen," he said. "Our whole way of life hangs in the balance, gentlemen."

That big, huh? thought Ruby.

* * *

At the depot Fitz-Hume was still roaring hellos into the phone and getting back a gentle purr. The bastards had hung up on them, and behind, the natives were getting restless.

— Sixteen —

Millbarge had taken the whole thing philosophically. He had bartered his shoelaces for a goat kebab and he was squatting in the crossroads watching the world go by and vaguely grinning at a puppet show.

A puppet donkey was kicking shit out of a little guy in a Russian uniform. The puppeteers dangled the donkey and the Russian, happily grinning back at Millbarge and nudging one another behind their cardboard stage. They had never seen a tourist but they had instincts and they reckoned Millbarge might be worth a month's wages.

Fitz-Hume, by comparison, was still furious. On the way back from the telephone, he had been approached by an old man with a monkey on his shoulder. The old man wanted alms or something. Maybe he wanted to tell

Fitz-Hume's fortune. Fitz-Hume neither knew nor cared. He hardly broke stride as he glanced at the monkey and said to the old man: "No, thanks. I've eaten already."

And the sight of Millbarge's complacent, cud-chewing face didn't help. He told him what Ruby had said.

"Pamir?" Millbarge said, chewing goat. "Dushanbe? Are you sure that's what he said?"

"Right. Those places are in Russia, aren't they?" They sounded kind of Russian.

"And how," said Millbarge.

"So. How can we get there? It must be a thousand miles from here."

Millbarge squinted at the signpost by the bus station. "Actually this is the Bunji province. Which means we're only about a hundred and fifty miles from the Soviet border."

Millbarge's all-embracing knowledge of trivia was beginning to piss Fitz-Hume off. He told him so.

"You would have to know. How can we possibly get across?"

Millbarge burped goat meat and stated the obvious. "We don't shave. We sell our clothes. We sell the ambulance and we go native."

Easy. Fitz-Hume wondered why he hadn't thought of it.

An hour later, dressed in furs, they were on an up-country bus and suffering. Fitz-Hume was a native New Yorker. He knew about bad travel. He'd been brought up on the subway and the bucking buses, but this thing made a crosstown bus seem like a stretch limo.

They were surrounded and suffocating. People clambered all over them. Goats and chickens made a lot of noise and smell. A number of times he thought he was about to pass out, but each time a tiny gap appeared in the furry mass of humanity and he took a lungful.

What he needed was a blast of good old Washington carbon monoxide.

"How far do we have to go in this bus?" he grumbled.

"As far as it takes us," said Millbarge.

Fitz-Hume sulked. He sneaked a glance at Millbarge, who was standing swaying, eyes half closed, leaning against a case of chickens. He looked as though he hadn't a care in the world and for a moment Fitz-Hume wanted to punch him on the nose. The man was so stuffed with morality. He wanted to get ahead by using the proper procedures, which made him a dangerous accomplice.

He was too conscientious by half. The man could get them both killed.

A noise behind made him turn. A land rover was gaining on them. He glanced idly at it, the only other vehicle he had seen; then he stiffened as it overtook them. He grabbed Millbarge's arm and pointed.

"Hey. That was Dr. Boyer."

Millbarge groaned. "She's the last person we want to see," he said.

"No. She was nice."

Millbarge shook his head and watched as Fitz-Hume fought his way up the bus, furs flapping, to get another look, disrupting chickens, creating a fuss. Millbarge made a mental note to write a memo about him when they got back. The man was irrational and therefore dangerous, breaking a fundamental law of espionage by drawing attention to himself.

Sometimes Millbarge wondered if Fitz-Hume knew even the basics of the business. Sometimes he wondered if the fool had even read Le Carré.

Three hours later the bus came to a merciful stop. The passengers got to their feet. Limbs creaked. Chickens squawked. A goat, in its excitement, peed on Millbarge's foot.

They were the first out, gulping dry air that tasted like champagne. But there was no sign of a café. Just a guard post, a barrier across the road manned by two men in uniform and a sign that read:

NORTHERN BUNJI TOLL

BUS 30,000
TRUCK 10,000
AUTO 5,000
CYCLES 1,000
PACK BEAST 100

Fitz-Hume stretched and yawned. "What's this?" he asked. "The border?"

Millbarge shook his head. "Toll stop. Hopefully there won't be any guard posts where we're going to cross."

Fitz-Hume yawned again. He was bored with all this. Then he saw something that made his boredom evaporate.

"Hey." He pointed. "There's Dr. Boyer."

Millbarge looked across the road. Behind the mass of humanity that had spilled off the bus, he saw the woman. She was dressed in a safari suit and a pith helmet and she was strapping something onto a pack mule. Millbarge squinted to get a better look. Among the luggage she was transferring from the land rover was a small metal case. Then he noticed her companion. It was Hadley.

He frowned, perplexed, then reached for Fitz-Hume who was moving toward them.

"Leave it alone," Millbarge said. But he was too late. Might as well try to stop a hippo in heat.

Fitz-Hume's eyes were bright with anticipation as he pushed through the crowd. He reached her just as she was climbing aboard the horse. He thought he had never seen anything so lovely. She was like a TV commercial for something.

"Hey," he said.

She looked down at him coldly. Glared, he thought, was the word. Certainly not friendly.

"I left without saying good-bye," he said. "Can you ever forgive me?"

In reply, she swung the mule's head around and kicked its haunches. The beast began to move away.

"Wait," he yelled. "Where are you going?"

She ignored him as he trotted behind her.

"You can't deny what happened back there between us," he shouted, reaching for her leg, thinking to pull her off if she did not stop.

She turned and looked down at him. Her nostrils quivered. Contempt oozed out of every pore.

"Don't touch me," she said.

He blinked in astonishment, then stood transfixed as she rode out of his life.

He couldn't believe it. He had never been rejected like that. Not since that singles bar in New York. What had happened? He turned, perplexed, and went in search of Millbarge.

The big man was at peace, squatting in the dirt chewing a kebab.

"How do you like that?" Fitz-Hume said, pointing up the road where Doctors Boyer and Hadley were now no more than specks in the distance. "She lets a little thing like death get in the way of romance."

Millbarge shook his head. "They couldn't have done any better with the Khan's brother than we did. They aren't doctors."

"Huh?"

"The metal case she packed onto her horse."

"What about it?"

"It's a Satscrambler terminal," said Millbarge, licking his fingers and chewing the last of the kebab. "It's a sophisticated system for sending, scrambling, receiving, and unscrambling satellite messages."

"So?" said Fitz-Hume. "She's a sophisticated woman."

Millbarge shook his head. "It's a piece of highly classified intelligence hardware."

"So," Fitz-Hume persisted. "She's a high-class, intelligent piece." Then the penny dropped. "You mean," he said, "they're spies like us?"

"Yes, they're spies, but not necessarily on our side."

Fitz-Hume nodded to himself. That explained it. That was why she had just given him a body swerve. Then he frowned, perplexed again. Then why had she come on to him when she thought he was a doctor? Maybe she had some kind of doctor-nurse fantasy. Who knows? Whatever it was, he was baffled, but he knew only one thing. He wasn't going to let her go.

"Well, I'd say it's our duty as American operatives to follow her and find out what she's up to."

"You just want to follow her," Millbarge said. "You're thinking with your dick."

"Look," Fitz-Hume persisted. "They left their land rover. They're probably going right across the border at a secret point. It would save us a lot of trouble."

Millbarge squinted at the horizon and nodded. "They do seem to be heading in that general direction," he conceded. "Maybe your dick's not so dumb."

"It got me through high school."

Millbarge thought for a moment, then came to a decision. "Well, let's go. We have to find a means of transportation, a camel or something."

Fitz-Hume shook his head. Camels belonged in zoos. And they were bad-tempered. He'd read about camels. The hell with camels.

—Seventeen—

It took Millbarge a long time to get his camel. The problem was the owner felt obliged to haggle. Millbarge didn't want to haggle. He had plenty of money from the sale of the ambulance, and besides, he was on expenses.

Eventually the deal was made. Then came the task of getting Fitz-Hume on the animal's back. He didn't want to do it. The camel didn't want to do it, but eventually Fitz-Hume was persuaded by the fact that Dr. Boyer had disappeared over the rim of the hill.

Millbarge sat in front with the reins, Fitz-Hume precariously perched behind him, grumbling, asking Millbarge why he had bought even more furs, in this heat. Millbarge ignored him and concentrated on getting the beast to go in the right direction. He kicked it but the camel was in no hurry.

It took them half an hour to reach the top of the hill. In the distance they could see the others. They were well mounted, a horse each and the pack mule. He hit the camel on its head and hurt himself. The camel responded by walking even slower.

"We're losing them," Fitz-Hume complained.

"I'm gouging with my heels as hard as I can," said Millbarge. "His fur is so thick he can't feel it."

Fitz-Hume swore. Millbarge told him to shut up. The camel belched. In the distance, the figures grew smaller. . . .

They had traveled for four hours and it seemed like a week. Millbarge was regretting the kebab but there was nothing he could do about it. They hadn't been supplied with a medical kit. His thighs ached from trying to drive the camel. It was a contrary beast and occasionally decided to go its own way, to make some kind of east-west detour, and there was nothing he could do about that either.

Plus, he was getting sick of Fitz-Hume's complaints.

Then the situation resolved itself. The camel stopped and farted, long and loud. Its head dropped, it kneeled on its forelegs, almost throwing them off, then settled on its haunches and gave a contented sigh.

"Did you say sit?" Fitz-Hume yelled.

"I didn't say sit," said Millbarge. "Did you say sit?"

"No."

Millbarge kicked, prodded, swiped, but the camel would not get up. What was worse, it started bellowing, lips drawn back, showing yellow teeth.

They got off fast. Fitz-Hume tried to out-bellow the beast but failed. He tried to out-stare it and failed. Then he put his face next to it and they roared at one another, camel and American. This time Fitz-Hume won. The camel turned away with a look of disgust.

Fitz-Hume's breath, thought Millbarge, must be bad.

Fitz-Hume turned in triumph. "Now what?" he asked.

Millbarge was already unloading their packs. "I guess we walk," he said.

In the distance the others were tiny specks climbing slowly. Beyond, they could see a range of white mountains.

Fitz-Hume began to walk, staggering under the weight of his pack and grumbling. "Why do we have to carry all this stuff?" he wanted to know.

Millbarge pointed. "The Dushanbe road runs across the top of the Pamir Mountains. The roof of the world." He tapped Fitz-Hume's pack and smiled. "You'll thank me later."

Oh yeah, Fitz-Hume thought, and pigs will fly.

*   *   *

In the bunker, the pace of activity was increasing by the hour. Every screen was a mass of data, every panel a jumble of equations. The fingers of the technicians danced on the keyboards, working fast and efficiently. There was no chaos, no frenzy. They were well trained and organized. Each man and woman knew the job backwards.

There was not an IQ in the place below 180.

Miegs and Sline, Ruby and Keyes lounged in their swivel chairs as if they were taking brandy in their clubs, but the atmosphere of relaxation was false.

Each stomach was a cauldron of tension. Veins throbbed in their temples. Fingers were clenched and unclenched.

To break the silence Keyes turned to Sline. "What was the final price of this system?"

"Just under sixty billion dollars."

"Quite a bargain," said Miegs.

Keyes nodded, tried to think of another thing to say but was interrupted by the arrival of one of the technicians, who handed a piece of paper to Sline.

"Printout from Gravsat, sir."

Sline took it. "Let's see. It's a transmission from the field." He looked at Keyes. "Your GIG-20s." And handed it over.

Keyes was relieved as he read it. "Wonderful," he breathed. "They confirm estimated arrival at the strike site by 6 P.M. their time tomorrow."

"That's 9 A.M. here," said Miegs. "Right on schedule."

Keyes felt his stomach begin to unknot. "You can always count on our people," he said happily.

—Eighteen—

They had left the plains behind and climbed. Thousands and thousands of feet through ascending barriers, to the snowline and beyond. Ever upward.

In an afternoon they had exchanged summer for the depths of winter. They turned and looked back the way they had come. The heat haze of the desert shimmered below and they shivered above.

It was time for winter clothing. Millbarge didn't look at Fitz-Hume as they unpacked, didn't want to shame him into an apology. He wasn't disappointed. He got no apology.

Ever upward. Snow tickled their ankles then sucked at their thighs. They reached the treeline and ploughed on, walking for an hour, maybe two, Fitz-Hume in the lead, and now it was dark. There was no light in the forest. They could hardly see a yard ahead.

"Wait, I've got to stop," Fitz-Hume said. "I'm exhausted. I've lost her for good."

Millbarge's patience snapped. "You're still thinking about that woman. I'm worrying about our general overall survival. Just keep walking."

"I can't."

"Why not?"

"Because there's nothing under my foot."

Millbarge gaped at him and then down. He gasped. Another step and Fitz-Hume would have tumbled over a precipice. Now he simply stood where he was, frozen in body and mind with cold and terror, one foot on earth and the other in midair, poised between life and death, heaven or hell.

Millbarge pulled him back.

Saved his life.

Fitz-Hume fell gratefully into the snow and closed his eyes. He owed Millbarge now. He opened his eyes to find Millbarge tugging at his sleeve and pointing.

Over the rim of the precipice, maybe a hundred yards down, they could see a road. A convoy of trucks slowly made its way along it, dozens of trucks, seemingly endless.

"The Dushanbe road," Millbarge whispered.

Then he was up and stumbling along the ridge to a spot where he could get down, with Fitz-Hume reluctantly following him. He would rather be anywhere else right now, but there was nowhere else to go.

Ten minutes later they were standing by the side of the road, ten yards back, out of sight among the trees.

"Well, this is it," Fitz-Hume whispered. "Where are these contacts we've heard so much about?"

"They didn't exactly say where on the road, did they?"

"No." Then Fitz-Hume had another brainstorm. "Maybe we should start hitchhiking."

Millbarge looked at him, adopted the tone again, the talking-to-a-child tone. "We're inside the Soviet Union."

Fitz-Hume pouted. "I wish we hadn't lost Boyer."

"They were on horseback," Millbarge whispered, exasperated now. "We had a camel."

He was seriously thinking of hitting Fitz-Hume when, without warning, lights came on, sweeping the area. They stepped back into the protection of the trees and clung to one another. Babes in the wood again.

Millbarge shaded his eyes and could make out the contours of what looked like a 1957 Chevy. It was almost a Chevy, he thought. But not quite. A Zill copy. And Zill was Russian. On its roof was a rack of spotlights, moving, searching for something.

A crackle of static, then an adenoidal voice spluttering something over a radio.

"What's he say?" Fitz-Hume whispered.

"It's the Tadzhik highway patrol. They were just sitting there. They heard our conversation."

Another stream of static and adenoids.

"What?" Fitz-Hume breathed.

"He said we needn't bother whispering." The lights found them and they blinked in the glare. "Come on," Millbarge said. "Let's get out of here."

Fitz-Hume peered through the beam, seeing the silhouettes of two men with guns, aiming at them.

"What do you mean, come on?" he squeaked. "We try that and they'll cut us down."

Millbarge shook his head. "We can't just go with them."

Procedure again, Fitz-Hume thought. The man always wants to do things by the book. The Russians were shouting at them now.

"What other choice do we have?" Fitz-Hume said. "At least if we give ourselves up, the state department can work out an exchange to get us home."

Russian boots crunched snow. They were getting impatient.

"Not me," said Millbarge, and he was gone. Fitz-Hume swiveled, caught sight of him flipping over backwards into the ditch and scrambling down the slope, then the Russians opened fire, simultaneous volleys, lighting up the darkness, bullets taking chunks off the trees.

Fitz-Hume's hands shot up as if pulled

by wires. The Russians stopped firing, came toward him, and now he could make out their faces under their fur hats—brutal, battered faces. Not a lot of humor there, he thought.

"Hi," he said, smiling at them, kind of friendly, as if he'd just stopped by to borrow some sugar. "It's okay. It's just me."

Fitz-Hume was quietly confident. The last state-department paper he had really paid any attention to was the one on the Geneva Convention, about the treatment of prisoners. He knew the exact date the Soviets had signed it.

"Just me," he said again.

Gunfire deafened him. Automatic-pistol fire lit up the forest. Bullets buzzed. It was like being in the middle of a beehive.

Fitz-Hume, as he dived for cover, became, in that moment, a cynical man. Geneva Convention, my ass, he said into the snow.

And from the depths of the forest he thought he heard a squeal, the sound of something furry dying.

The jailhouse was ten feet square, just a small table, two chairs, and a lamp shining in Fitz-Hume's face. The only concession to personal taste were tattered movie posters, of *Dr. Zhivago* and *Reds*.

Fitz-Hume was tied to a chair, his hands lashed by rope on his lap, a foul-smelling soldier barking questions in his ear. At least,

he assumed they were questions. He didn't
have a word of Russian. All he knew was
that the man had recently been eating cab-
bage.

The Russian paused, waiting for an answer, and Fitz-Hume, inspired by the posters, gave him what he thought he wanted.

"I was looking for the Burt Reynolds Dinner Theater."

The second Russian grunted and launched
into a monologue. When he had finished,
Fitz-Hume glared at him. He'd had enough
of being friendly. Now was the time to show
indignation, to demand his rights.

"Listen. I think I am entitled to a phone
call."

The door was flung open and the two Tab
Hunters strode in. But now they were dressed
in furs. Schnelker had obviously been listening.

"And who do you intend to call?" he asked.

Fitz-Hume groaned. He was in trouble. He
could tell by Schnelker's accent. The man
had dropped the West Coast drawl and lapsed
into the Russian of Central Casting, all adenoidal menace.

They seemed to fill the room. Hodges
backheeled the door shut. It closed with what
seemed to Fitz-Hume to be a terminal bang,
and just for a moment he gave in to despair.
He wished that Millbarge was around.

— *Nineteen* —

Millbarge awoke in a snow hole. He was warm
and comfortable and wanted to stay put. But
he knew from the survival booklets that it
was all illusion. Go to sleep again and maybe
you don't wake up this time.

He yawned and congratulated himself on
his escape. He had been lucky. He'd heard
the bullets whine around his ears, he'd seen
branches shattered by the automatic fire but
he had stumbled on, running fast through
the snow as if it were the track at a health
club.

He'd run faster and for a longer time than
he had since he was a kid. Half an hour
maybe. There was a proverb for it. Fear had
lent him wings. Or snow shoes. Something
like that.

Then he had collapsed in a drift. Vaguely

134

he remembered digging in. Now it was tomorrow and a new set of problems. He
dragged himself to his feet and trudged forward, not knowing where he was going, which
direction to take, or what to do. All he knew
was that he had to keep on the move.

He kept on the move for hours, stumbling
through drifts, walking blind, unaware that
he was walking in circles. Then he stopped,
his heart battering his ribs as he heard the
sound of gunfire. It was close. Far too close
for comfort. Part of him wanted to run from
it, but his curiosity proved to be more powerful than fear. Slowly, bent double, he moved
forward. The firing had stopped. Maybe it
had been for Fitz-Hume.

Dawn was the traditional time, wasn't it?
And sadness flooded through him, surpris-
ing in its intensity. Poor Emmett. The man
was a nitwit—devious, cowardly and lech-
erous—but he didn't deserve a Russian firing squad. Not just for cheating on an exam.

Then the horizon tilted. He was in midair
and tumbling. There was nothing under his
feet. He yelled, arms flailing, eyes tightly
shut, then hit snow and slithered, head over
heels, trying to find a grip, cursing himself
for worrying about Fitz-Hume in a forest
full of hidden gullies.

Then something stopped him, something
furry and warm and sticky.

He opened his eyes and stared into the
face of Hadley. He was a corpse. The corpse

stared back at him. Millbarge whimpered. His left hand was warm with the man's blood. He threw himself into the snow and shuddered. The man's chest had been shattered by bullets.

Millbarge sat and shivered, gazed around him. Three more bodies lay a few yards away, all in gray uniforms, two stretched out, one huddled like a fetus, each one staining the snow with blood.

Millbarge retched. He had never seen death. He wouldn't have seen this carnage if it weren't for his morbid curiosity. Then he heard something move. The noise came from the trees about fifty yards away.

He got up and walked slowly toward it. Curiosity again. It would be the death of him, he thought.

He saw Boyer before she saw him, a bundle of furs against a tree. As he approached, she turned and looked up at him, then raised a pistol and pointed it at his head.

"What are you doing here?" she said.

Millbarge stopped, staring at the pistol and trembling, throwing her question back at her: "What are *you* doing here?"

Boyer nodded toward the trio of corpses. "They surprised us," she said. "Border troops. They got my partner." She lowered the gun and he bent to help her to her feet.

"Looks like they got you too."

"I'm fine," she said.

Millbarge shook his head at the waste of

life around them. "No wonder none of you could do that appendix operation. You're spies like us. And I guess you're on our side. From the look of it."

Boyer blinked in surprise. "You mean you're . . . ?"

"Austin Millbarge," he said, shaking her free hand. "I'm a GLG-20."

Realization dawned. She nodded and chewed her bottom lip. "So, you two are the other GLG-20s. The decoys. You're the ones they told us would be out here to take the heat off us."

The news hit Millbarge like a punch in the belly. "Decoys?" he wheezed. "Us?"

Couldn't be, could it? No. Surely not. But Boyer continued nodding like some toy in the back of a car and suddenly everything fell into place.

"So that's why they rushed us through training, why we were met by the KGB. They sent us right into enemy hands."

"Right," said Boyer as if this sort of thing happened every day. "But it wasn't supposed to happen to us . . . the main team."

Millbarge was instantly puffed full of indignation. He stamped his foot in a snow-drift. "I'm extremely pissed off," he said. "My friend and I were set up."

"Forget it," said Boyer. "That's behind us now. We have to cover the bodies and establish a base camp. We have a project to complete."

"Project!" Millbarge yelled, hardly able to believe what he was hearing. Project, my ass, he thought. Suddenly he knew exactly where his loyalties lay. "Fitz-Hume is in the custody of the Tadzhik highway patrol because of you," he said. "The only project right now is to get my partner out."

—*Twenty*—

Fitz-Hume had been awake all night. They wouldn't let him sleep, kept shining lights in his face and prodding him. If he'd told them once, he'd told them a thousand times that they would pay for this. You don't fool around with one of the sons of Uncle Sam, no sir, he had told them, but they didn't seem to worry much.

There was no feeling in his hands and he was frightened, but at least they hadn't turned violent and he was glad of that. Violence was old-fashioned these days. So one of the state-department papers had said. He could only hope that they had read it.

Since dawn Schnelker and Hodges had been asking him stupid questions and he was getting sick and tired of giving the same answers.

Now it was the turn of Hodges, while Schnelker stood by the door, practicing his menacing look. Fitz-Hume wasn't impressed. A child could look menacing to someone lashed to a chair with his hands tied. Didn't take much practice.

"Why are you here?" Hodges spat at him.

"I've been asking myself the same thing," he said.

"What is your objective?"

"My objective?" He thought for a moment, then smiled. "I object to taking a girl out, buying her dinner, and then she doesn't put out."

He snickered. He quite liked his little joke. But Hodges didn't laugh. Maybe he didn't understand what *put out* meant. They probably told him in Moscow it was something to do with cats.

"Why are you here?" Hodges muttered.

"Why am I here? Why are you here? Why is anyone here? It was Jean-Paul Sartre who once said: 'How do you spell Sartre?' "

Schnelker growled at this, stepped across the room, and slapped him hard on the cheek. It stung. Fitz-Hume growled back: "All right, that's it. Now I'm getting mad."

He turned the other cheek and got a second slap. Harder this time.

"And let that be a lesson to you," Fitz-Hume shouted, then he began to tremble as he saw Hodges draw a hunting knife from a sheath on his belt. It gleamed. It was curved. It looked pretty sharp.

"Every minute you don't tell us why you're here," Hodges said with a grin, "I cut off a finger."

"Mine or yours?" Fitz-Hume just couldn't resist it.

"Yours."

"Damn."

Schnelker slapped him again and Fitz-Hume yelled: "Hey. What are you still hitting me for? He's gonna cut off my fingers."

"You have thirty seconds," said Hodges.

Fitz-Hume was scared now. "You're not going to hum the 'Jeopardy' theme, are you?" he asked. That was all he needed right now.

"We'll start with a little one," said Hodges as Schnelker untied Fitz-Hume's right hand, slapped it on the table, and held it down. Still Fitz-Hume could feel nothing, which was a small mercy. Hodges spat on the blade and pulled the dead little finger and Fitz-Hume had a flash of memory. The Khan's brother. The scalpel. The heart attack.

"All right, all right," he yelled. "I'm an American agent."

"And?" said Hodges.

"And I'm here to"—he scrambled for an idea—"to assassinate your premier."

"I knew it," said Hodges, laughing happily, slapping his thigh, grinning at Schnelker, hand held out. "Pay up."

Schnelker pouted and drew out a wad of

rubles, counted a few off the top, and handed them over. He didn't like losing bets and now he was mean.

"Let's cut off his fingers anyway," he suggested.

"No," said Hodges. "Let's take him back to headquarters in Moscow."

"Good move," said Fitz-Hume.

That decided, they untied him and helped him to his feet, walked him round the room for a couple of minutes till the blood had returned to his legs and feet, then hand-cuffed him and pushed him toward the door. Schnelker went first, Hodges bringing up the rear.

Fitz-Hume took a last look at his prison, thinking of Moscow. It wasn't much of a place by all accounts but it had to be better than this. At least he'd be able to get a call to the embassy.

Surely they'd allow him that. Then the wheels of diplomacy would start to turn. He'd make the *Washington Post*. Maybe even *Time* and *Newsweek*. Maybe even the cover?

As Hodges shoved him out, Fitz-Hume wondered how many Russians he'd be traded for. Ten. Maybe twenty. Then he'd know for sure how important he was considered.

The Zill was parked in the snow a few yards away. Fitz-Hume gulped mountain air and glanced around him. The place was beautiful. Pines and little fir trees stretching down the slopes toward the desert. Not a cloud in the sky. Perfect for a vacation. If it was in Vermont.

Then he blinked. Coming toward him was a mirage, something out of a western. A man in furs, galloping toward them, strapped into the saddle, two pistols in his hand— someone who looked remarkably like Austin Millbarge.

Flashes from the pistols, followed a millisecond later by the crackle of gunfire, then Schnelker and Hodges were diving for cover.

It *was* Millbarge. A one-man seventh cavalry. Fitz-Hume was amazed. He never knew that the man could ride a horse like that. Must have read how to up in his apartment.

The big horse kept galloping toward him while Millbarge yelled like a banshee, sending bullets everywhere, ripping into the blockhouse, stitching up the Zill.

Fitz-Hume knew exactly what to do. He raised his handcuffed hands and thought back to the Saturday matinees. Just hook the handcuffs over the pommel and swing up onto the horse behind Millbarge. It was easy. Except it wasn't Saturday and he had never been much good at anything athletic.

The horse skidded to a halt, Fitz-Hume grabbed the pommel. The horse took off. Fitz-Hume vaulted for the saddle, missed and dragged it off, Millbarge with it, a jumble of arms and legs in the snow, the horse whinnying and trotting away.

They got up fast and so did Schnelker and

Hodges and the two cops, all of whom were leveling their guns at them.

There was a pile of logs behind them, three feet high. They vaulted it as the bullets zipped around their ears and into the logs, sending splinters ten feet high.

Fitz-Hume cowered, then looked at his hands. They were free. The handcuffs had been severed by a bullet. He gazed at the broken chain, then up, in wonderment, at Millbarge.

"Did you do that?"

"Yeah," Millbarge said. "I did it for you." Then he stood up and fired, double-fisted, and Schnelker and Hodges ducked behind the Zill, while the cops ran for the blockhouse.

Now it was shoot-out time. Millbarge handed Fitz-Hume a pistol, told him it was a MAC-10. Fitz-Hume shrugged. He'd always spent the mandatory firearm classes with Alice. Now he wished he hadn't. He stood up and fired and hurt himself. Schnelker and Hodges fired back. He sat again and watched Millbarge reloading.

"I must like you," Millbarge said. "Because I don't like horses and I hate guns."

It was the nicest thing anyone had ever said to him. Zip. Whine. Ricochet. They were under savage attack. They cowered behind their wall of logs, watching it gradually disintegrate. They were outnumbered. Soon they would be without any cover. It was time to think of something.

A clink and something bounced into Fitz-Hume's lap, a small, black, shiny piece of metal, the size of a baseball, with a handle attached. He picked it up and looked at it curiously.

"What's this?" he asked.

Millbarge stared at it, bug-eyed, hair on end. "You don't want it," he whispered.

Fitz-Hume shrugged, got to his feet, aimed at the window of the blockhouse and pitched the thing back, just like he once did in the Little League.

For a moment there was silence. Suspended animation. The Russians were reloading. Then the blockhouse door opened and the two cops ran out, scrambling up the slope, running faster than deer, for they knew something that Fitz-Hume didn't. That the little black baseball was a grenade. High-explosive. That Fitz-Hume had pitched it into a box of twenty other high-explosive grenades. That the release time was ten seconds.

The blockhouse exploded with a *whump* that blasted the eardrums of all six men. Then again, an echo from the mountains, starting avalanches, frightening the horse.

Millbarge was the first to react, grabbing Fitz-Hume, running to the horse, calming it, leaping onto its bare back, dragging Fitz-Hume after him.

This time Fitz-Hume made it. All he needed, he reckoned, was a bit of practice, fueled by terror.

"Heigho, Silver," he yelled as bullets began zipping past his head again. But now he felt invincible. He turned and saw Schnelker and Hodges, fifty yards behind, knees bent, their guns held double-fisted in the classic firing position. He stuck his tongue out at them.

They fired. He felt something sizzle past his ear, then the horse was in full gallop, leaving the Russians helpless.

Siberia for them, Fitz-Hume thought happily. The salt mines this time. Definitely, and maybe a few sadistic jailers who enjoyed chopping off fingers.

— *Twenty-one* —

Karen Boyer didn't even look up as they rode in, Millbarge shouting: "We're back."

She was too busy, bent over the scrambler. She had set it up in the snow, a small receiving dish pointing at the sky, westward. The machine bleeped and whirred and Boyer frowned in concentration.

Fitz-Hume was first to dismount. He had a bone to pick with this woman.

"Hey," he said, tapping her shoulder. "What's this about us just being decoys? You know those guys were going to cut off my finger?"

"Wait," she said, shushing him. "I'm sending."

Fitz-Hume's anger melted at the sound of her voice. He looked dreamily at Millbarge.

"I think she's beautiful," he said.

But Millbarge was less patient. He wasn't in love. He wanted answers.

"What were you sending on that Sat scrambler? I demand to know who's running this operation. Is it ARPA? DOS? DCI? DOD? DIA?"

"There's no time," she said, getting to her feet. "We're three hours away from the Go code."

"The Go code for what?" Millbarge asked.

"I'm sorry. Those orders are classified until we reach the final objective."

Fitz-Hume butted in. "What *is* the final objective?"

"I don't know," she said, "but according to this"—she held up a strip of printed paper from the machine—"it's only about half a mile from here. Over that ridge."

She pointed north, snapped the machine shut, got to her feet, and set off toward the ridge, leading the pack mule. Millbarge shook his head, planted his feet firmly in the snow, and folded his arms. "I'm not going one step further until I know what's going on," he said.

Fitz-Hume, in a dilemma, grabbed his arms and pleaded with him: "Austin, please. For me. I'm getting in good with her again. I can feel it. Come on, man. It's only half a mile."

They trudged through the snow, Boyer in the lead, and they were almost at the top when Millbarge grabbed her arm.

"Listen," he whispered. "You hear something?"

She shook her head. The fur hat acted as earplugs but Fitz-Hume could hear it. Something drifting up from the gully below, something vaguely familiar.

"Yeah," said Fitz-Hume. "What is it?"

"It sounds like music," Millbarge said.

"It is," Fitz-Hume said, moving forward, one hand behind his ear, the rhythm of "Soul Finger" throbbing beneath his feet. "It's the Barkays."

Fitz-Hume shrugged. "I always wondered what happened to them. I guess they're still having trouble getting good gigs."

They dropped to their knees and crawled the remaining few yards to the top and peered over. "Soul Finger" drifted up to them and in the gully below, thirty yards away, they saw the source of the music. It was a massive ghetto blaster, beside a campfire, and three ghostly figures, dressed in white, breakdancing enthusiastically around it.

Tents had been pitched around the fire but the attention of Fitz-Hume, Millbarge, and Boyer was riveted to the massive camouflaged tractor parked beyond the fire.

"Wow," said Millbarge, entranced. "That's an SS-50 mobile launcher and long-range rocket." Never, in his wildest dreams, had he ever thought he would see such a thing, and he felt privileged. No other American could ever claim to have seen one, not in the flesh, as it were.

"This is a Soviet ICBM site," Boyer said.

"And they must have just moved it in here," Millbarge added. "They haven't even put up their locator beacon. That means they're not hooked into the Soviet defense chain yet."

"Only three men," Boyer said.

Just then a tent flap opened and a woman came out. A woman like a shot-putter. She flapped her hand at the music and the men meekly stopped dancing and switched off the cassette.

"And their mother," said Fitz-Hume.

Another flap opened and another woman emerged. A very different woman. Her white suit was open to the waist, revealing an amazing body. Great big firm breasts, brown against the background of the snow.

Millbarge gasped. "Oh, look what just stepped out."

"Where are those binoculars?" said Fitz-Hume as she started zipping up.

Millbarge had them. He was peering through them. "I'm in love," he said.

"Let me see," said Fitz-Hume.

"Wait a minute." said Millbarge. The zipper had stuck momentarily. He squirmed in the snow and gurgled.

"Come on," said Fitz-Hume impatiently, vaguely aware that already he was being mentally unfaithful to Boyer. But he didn't care.

"Okay, okay," Millbarge said, handing the binoculars over but taking care to keep the strap around his neck.

Fitz-Hume's hands shook as he gazed down. She had zipped up now and was adjusting her hood. It was designed for arctic conditions: only the eyes, nose, and mouth were visible, but it was enough.

"That's enough," Millbarge said. "She's mine."

They fought, slapping wrists, until Boyer brought them back to earth.

"Honestly," she said. "You two are unbelievable."

Millbarge nodded in agreement. "Hold it," he said. "Wait a minute. What are we doing here?"

"This is our final objective," Boyer said. "Our project orders are to subdue the crew and seize control of the emplacement."

"What for?" asked Fitz-Hume.

"An intelligence and technical appraisal, I guess. They'll tell us in the next signal from Gravsat."

Millbarge took another look at the trailer and shook his head. "Hold it, sister," he said. "We're not going near that thing. That missile is tipped with a forty-megaton fission-fusion nuclear warhead."

That was enough for Fitz-Hume. He got to his feet and wished everyone good-bye.

"Where are you going?" Boyer asked.

"Home."

Millbarge dragged his eyes away from the young woman and nodded at Boyer. "For once I'm in complete agreement with my friend," he said. "I think we should all get up and leave this place immediately."

Boyer opened her mouth to protest and Millbarge pointed to the tractor and its load. "You know what that thing can do? Suck the paint off houses and give your family permanent orange Afros."

"Right," said Fitz-Hume. "How do we get out of here?"

"Only after we've seized the emplacement will our controllers transmit our safe-route-to-home coordinates," Boyer said.

Millbarge groaned. "They would build a clause like that into the deal," he grumbled.

"Look," said Boyer, hands on hips, reminding Fitz-Hume of Alice. "I don't care what you two do, I'm fulfilling my obligation. I intend to go down there and seize that emplacement. Alone if I have to."

This was crafty; an appeal to their better nature, but Fitz-Hume wasn't buying.

"You know we'd do anything in the world for you," he said. "But we can't seize the rocket. We'd have to kill everybody down there."

Millbarge nodded emphatically. "And I'm not killing anyone."

For a moment there was silence. A stand off. Then Boyer spoke slowly and carefully, looking first at one, then the other.

"Gentlemen, I think you both should realize the gravity of this moment. I have spent two and a half years of my life preparing for this penetration. This afternoon I buried my partner, Gerry Hadley, perhaps the finest, most dedicated GLG-20 in the history of the service."

Her voice trembled and she paused, bit her lip, and Fitz-Hume wanted her to cry so that he could take her in his arms and brush away her tears. He felt protective. It was a completely new sensation.

"Gerry's forever entombed in a snowy grave," she continued, "and it's not going to be for nothing." She nodded in determination and stood as if to attention. "We are here today to help guarantee the freedom of every American," she said. "We must never forget the words of President John F. Kennedy: 'Ask not what your country can do for you, but what you can do for your country.'"

Millbarge sniffed, thought he was going to cry.

Fitz-Hume was overcome, gazing at Boyer in adoration. "Will you marry me?" he whispered, but she ignored him, walked over to the mule, unstrapped a small case and opened it. Inside, nestling in velvet, were two wide-barreled handguns.

For a terrible moment Millbarge thought he was going to have to fight a duel or something. But no.

"These are high-compression tranquilizer

pistols," she said. "We're not killing anybody, but we've got to get close to use them."

They were going to have to become heroes. There was no other option.

— Twenty-two —

In the bunker, nails had been bitten down below the pain threshold and the tension was almost visible.

A technician tapped his keyboard and announced: "Hours T minus two until designated apogee."

Lights flashed, green, yellow, pink. Like a discotheque without the music, Ruby thought. He was perspiring and chewing his lip and wondering what the hell was going on up there in the outside world.

"Sir," said a second technician, turning to Miegs. "All air traffic has been diverted from our response corridor."

"What's our present on-line power reading?" Miegs asked.

"Michigan reactors and Washington State atomic plants coming on line, General."

Sline nodded and cracked his knuckles. "Lock us in, soldier," he said.

Fingers danced on the keyboard and through the underground maze, three-inch thick steel doors dropped from the roof, closing off sections of corridor. A steward, pushing a drinks trolley, was whistling happily when a door dropped in front of him. He turned. Another closed behind him with a clang of finality. He was trapped. He looked at his cargo of Pepsi, orange juice, and lemonade and slowly subsided into sobs.

In the command post a technician was announcing: "WAMP secure, sir."

"Let's go to Response Level Yellow," Sline said. "Run your full servo and arming."

Ruby gazed at him, reluctantly impressed. He hadn't a clue what the man was talking about. But the technician understood.

"Initiating Level Yellow," he said, leaning across his console to two switches marked SERVO ASSIST and ARM TIP. The switches were locked in by two levers. Unhesitatingly he snapped them back, revealing two red pulsing bulbs, an inch in diameter. Beneath the bulbs, two locks.

Ruby watched the man closely as he produced a key, placed it in the first lock and turned it, then another key in the second lock. The man was totally emotionless. He was as programmed for action as the machinery he was awakening.

The earth began to move. Enormous pul-

leys took the strain. Servo-pistons thrust
themselves up through greased barrels. On
the surface the desert vibrated, sending a
cloud of dust into the heat haze.

Slowly, as it had been programmed, the
roof of the projector blockhouse of the Lancaster Drive-in 3 split in half, drawn by pul-
leys, sliding back on oiled hinges. The operation took exactly two minutes, then from the
depths of the building, three black metallic
phalluses emerged, glistening, pointing at
the sky, their tips fringed with antennae.
They thrust eight feet above the blockhouse
roof, then stopped and clicked into place.

Ready for deployment, humming and throbbing, while deep below, its computerized brain
waited for the next instruction.

—*Twenty-three*—

They had to wait until the middle of the night. Boyer had told them so. Orders. Something to do with time differences. Fitz-Hume had a blasphemous thought. Maybe they were doing all this for the TV stations. Middle of the night here would be prime time back home.

But at least they had time to work out a plan.

It had been Fitz-Hume's idea to dress up for the part, and once he got going, he became quite inventive. It was he who thought of taking the silver foil from Boyer and Hadley's food parcels and tearing it into strips. It was he who thought of cannibalizing pieces of the scrambler to make colored beading. It was he who thought of fitting their flashlights under their collars so that they would

158

be lit up like a composite of the Halloween bogeyman and the Christmas fairy.

Millbarge added the clincher. Snow goggles to hide their eyes and give them an alien look.

And all this to the sound of "Soul Finger" drifting from the galley and the giggles of the beautiful crew member who had been dancing nonstop for an hour with each of the men in turn.

Now again a belch surfaced and Boyer, on watch, looked satisfied. Down below they were on their third bottle of vodka of the night.

Fitz-Hume felt more alive than he had in years. Maybe it was something to do with the saying about the prospect of imminent death sharpening the mind. Or maybe it was love, the thought that perhaps Boyer was looking upon him as heroic. He wasn't sure. He had never gone in for self-analysis. All he knew, as he climbed into his survival suit, was that he was excited. He even sang along with the Barkays.

Millbarge wasn't so sure. He grumbled as Fitz-Hume fixed the lights to his neck. The homemade antenna tickled his ears. He felt silly and wasn't at all sure that the idea would work. But he had to go along with it because he had not come up with anything better.

Then they were ready to go. Boyer had

already set the flares in the pine trees down to their left. She looked at them, then scuttled away. They gave her two minutes, then followed her down the slope out of sight of the Soviets. The plan was to make their way around the flank and then appear at the edge of the woods, ten yards from the campfire.

On the way down they practiced a stiff-legged, somnambulist walk, arms held stiffly out at their sides. It took them five minutes to reach their mark. For the moment they were hidden from the Soviets by the trees. The noise of "Soul Finger" was louder now. They could hear the gurgle of vodka as the biggest crewman poured it down his throat. They saw the beautiful one twitching to the rhythm and Millbarge had to look away. The survival suit was far too tight for the thoughts that crept into his mind.

Fitz-Hume turned, gave the thumbs-up sign to Boyer, who waved back, then lit the flares.

A whoosh and the sky was lit up. Pine branches crackled and burned. The Soviets spun around to watch, transfixed.

It was their cue. Center stage. Fame.

They switched on their flashlights, took deep breaths, and strode stiff-legged into the open.

The Soviets stared at them, then stepped back in terror, shielding their eyes, then stepped forward again, unslinging their rifles.

Millbarge whimpered. It wasn't going to work. They were going to be shot down wearing all this ludicrous fancy dress. It was such an undignified way to die; the only compensation at the moment of death was the sight of the young crew woman, backlit by a dying flare, in glorious silhouette.

They stopped twenty feet from the campfire as the shot-putt woman began to whisper to the men.

"What's she saying?" Fitz-Hume hissed.

"Hairbrush . . . headrest," Millbarge hissed back, straining to hear. "No, wait . . . barn . . . childhood . . . Lithuania . . . uncle . . . cow . . . elevator . . . energy . . . shotgun and barbecue."

"Where did you take your Russian courses?" asked Fitz-Hume. "J. C. Penney?"

"Wait. Listen. Comet . . . traveler . . . spit . . . fire . . . space shot . . ." He snapped his fingers. "I've got it. When she was a little girl in Lithuania at her uncle's farm, a spaceship landed and stole an ox her uncle had just shot for roasting."

"See, I knew this would work," whispered Fitz-Hume in triumph. "People everywhere know about UFOs and aliens."

"I don't think her experience with one was pleasant," Millbarge added. "She's saying they dissected the ox and kept the best pieces for themselves. The ox was to have fed her whole village for a week."

Fitz-Hume couldn't see the problem. "So what?" he said. "We owe her an ox."

Just then the big woman began advancing on them. She had balls, Millbarge thought, and a gun. She cocked it and motioned to the others to advance. Cautiously they moved closer. Millbarge began to whimper, but Fitz-Hume was prepared. He had a plan.

"Do exactly what I do," he whispered.

They were only a few yards away now. Fitz-Hume suddenly lurched sideways, grabbed his throat with both hands, gave out a rasping death rattle, flailed for air, spun a couple of times, then threw himself backwards into the snow and lay still.

The Soviets stopped, heads cocked like puppies.

Easy as pie, thought Millbarge, lurching sideways, grabbing his throat, rasping, flailing, spinning, and falling.

It was cold but they could not shiver, not when they were playing dead. The Soviets moved slowly forward until they were only a few feet away. Through half-closed lids, Millbarge and Fitz-Hume watched them, saw their curious expressions, heard the guns being raised.

Then the flames died out. It was now or never. As one, Fitz-Hume and Millbarge sat up, drew the pistols from their belts behind their backs and fired. Darts pierced the Soviet snowsuits. They fell backwards, instantly tranquilized, dreaming of home. A couple of fingers instinctively tightened on triggers and the rifles went off harmlessly into the air.

Then silence. Fitz-Hume and Millbarge got to their feet, checked the sleeping bodies, and grinned at one another.

Heroes. Reluctant heroes maybe, but heroes nonetheless.

In the bunker the message they had all been waiting for came through.

"Satscram signal from the strike site," said the technician. "Your GLG-20s have penetrated successfully and are awaiting the Go code."

Keyes winked at Miegs, both men feeling the tension drain out of them. Their people had done it. Their responsibility was over, their job done. Now they could relax. Whatever happened next was down to the military.

A technician checked his screen and announced: "All our *Hi-Weather* birds are confirming their bounce position."

Miegs nodded. "Open and lock down ground reflector."

Two more locks were opened. Keys were turned and above ground the drive-in screen slowly began to tilt backwards.

It took thirty seconds for the old screen to ease back onto the desert floor, pulling up the new screen as it went, something that would never show a movie, something that Harry Keyes, in the days when he watched

Hedy Lamarr, would never have thought possible.

This screen was thirty feet wide by twenty feet high, a mass of intermeshed reflective wafers, glinting green and blue in the desert sun.

It clicked into place a hundred yards due north of the old projector house where the three-pronged black projectile waited.

It was almost time.

—*Twenty-four*—

They could feel it. Excitement, apprehension, a sensation that they were at the epicenter of something colossal. Fitz-Hume was fantasizing about something old-fashioned, a ticker-tape welcome back home.

Millbarge was gazing at the sleeping young woman, wondering if, when all this was over, he could persuade her to defect to his apartment.

Boyer thought only of the machine in front of her, which was beginning to come to life, the first stuttering instructions inching out into her hand.

"The final signal's unscrambling now," she said, and the others crowded around her.

"Where does it say how we get home?" Fitz-Hume asked.

She frowned, trying to make sense of the

words. "This isn't the clear text I usually get," she said. "It's in code." She slapped her forehead in frustration. "They're being extra careful. They don't know about Hadley. He was the expert on codes."

Millbarge squinted at it, then grinned. "No problem," he said, ripping off the text. It was a simple enough code to him. Not to many others, but to him. He didn't even need his Drogan's wheel.

"Go on then, genius," Fitz-Hume said. "What does it say?"

"It says"—he squinted—"approach the Programmable Guidance SS-50 Long-Range Ballistic Missile."

Slowly they approached it, Millbarge leading, Fitz-Hume in the rear.

They stood for a moment in awe of it, gazing at the terrible length of it above them, each of them trying not to think of the power it carried in the nose cone. Ginger Afros, Millbarge had said. Yeah. They'd all seen the documentaries.

Millbarge checked the printout again. "Easy," he said. "Find the pull-out console beneath the front rear erector arm."

This was easy. It was obvious. Fitz-Hume and Boyer tenderly touched a hatch on the rocket and even more gently undid a couple of latches.

A panel dropped open, revealing a typewriter keyboard.

"This is a snap," said Millbarge, excited now, thinking only of finding out what was next. His curiosity was again taking over. He checked the printout and translated. "Turn on erector power source by switching on top two keys left."

He did it himself and stepped back as the thing came alive, purring deep in its intestines, the sound of a hundred contented pussycats.

"Enter the following sequence by individual letter key," Millbarge said, then dictated the letters to Boyer, who punched them in: "QQ—MM—T—O—B—AK—USA. Stop."

She stopped.

"Hold number sequence," he said. Then: "Acknowledge compliance on Satscram." The code demanded urgency. "NOW!" he yelled.

Boyer did as she was told, hitting the Satscram keyboard at her feet.

"Acknowledging compliance on Satscram now," she said.

Fitz-Hume, watching all this, felt slightly annoyed. Millbarge was being a little too dominant for comfort, and what was worse, Boyer was being far too passive.

In the bunker the instruments were all pulsing, throbbing their way toward some kind of electronic orgasm.

Miegs, Sline, Ruby, and Keyes were on their feet, staring at the head technician, their faces reflected as four ghosts in his video screen.

"Satscram signal coming in now," he said. "GS-20s acknowledge programming and compliance."

Sline twitched, a muscle in his jaw working overtime. "Let's move to Response Level Red," he said.

"Initiating Response Level Red," said the technician, hitting buttons. "Initiated and engaged."

"Bring all birds into final bounce mode," said Sline.

The technician did as he was told; fingers blurred on his keyboard, and above in the ionosphere, three complex pieces of technology obeyed his instructions.

From its orbit, two hundred miles above the Indian Ocean, a satellite shifted position and checked its coordinates. A panel in its port side slid open and a wafer-thin metallic arm unfolded; three right-angled joints, pointing earthward in anticipation of the next instruction from the nerve center a thousand feet beneath the Nevada desert.

A millisecond later, its sister satellite over the southern Pacific performed the same act, followed by a third over the southern mass of the U.S.A.: all three almost instantaneously locked into position, ready and waiting for their big moment.

In the bunker Miegs was ready.

"Send them the Go code," he said to the technician.

It was time.

Three seconds later, halfway across the world, the Satscrambler chattered again. The message was brief and made Boyer shiver. She had no need for Millbarge to translate. She knew this message by heart. It was branded into her memory. The Go code. The most exciting moment of her career.

She looked at Millbarge who was standing by the panel in the side of the rocket looking back at her expectantly.

"Go with numbered sequence," she said, ripping off the tape and handing it over.

"Numbered sequence," Millbarge repeated, his fingers reaching for the top line on the keyboard. "23—406—74—74—25—0—5—0—337."

As soon as he hit the seven, the rocket came to life. From its belly could be heard clicking and ticking as tumblers fell into place.

Instinctively Millbarge, Fitz-Hume, and Boyer stepped away from it, backing off fast as hydraulic pumps hissed and two erector arms beneath the launch platform went into action.

It took exactly eight seconds. A low rumble of ignition turned into a roar, smoke belched from the base of the rocket, and then the first flames. The rocket was pointing to the stars now, at its extreme angle.

Flames lit up the gully, snow sizzled and turned to steam. Pine trees caught fire, then the smoke blinded them. They automatically closed their eyes as the rocket began to move, and by the time they had opened them, it was gone, just a flickering flame above them, heading west, leaving a fifty-foot-diameter circle of blackened earth and burning pine.

"I think we just started World War Three," said Millbarge softly.

The Soviets were slowly coming to, staring at the sky. One of them reached for his rifle, then saw that his ammunition clip had been removed. Not that it mattered. Not now. The older woman let out a shriek and Millbarge translated it.

"She wants to know why we would do such a thing," he said.

"Tell her so do we," said Fitz-Hume.

"Oh my God," Boyer whispered. "It's going to be the end of the world."

Millbarge nodded, still curious. "Why would they want us to do such a thing?"

The Soviets had got to their feet and were chattering to one another.

"What are they saying?" Fitz-Hume asked.

"They're saying," said Millbarge, "that it'll take about twenty-eight minutes before that rocket hits its target inside the continental United States."

He looked at his watch. "It's now four-forty-seven A.M.," he said. "Twenty-eight minutes, which means it will be inside the U.S. radar cup in eighteen minutes, so our response should be about two minutes after that. That's twenty until total commitment, and ... let's see ... figure another twenty until total impact of the first warheads. I figure we have about forty-two minutes until the end of civilization as we know it."

All this was delivered unemotionally, in a monotone, as if he were reading the weather forecast.

Fitz-Hume felt numb. He couldn't grasp the enormity of what had happened. In that moment, the primitive part of him reared its head. He put his arm round Boyer and whispered: "Wanna go out with a bang?"

"I beg your pardon," she said.

"It was only a suggestion," he said.

Her eyes widened. She stared at him. He thought she was going to put her hands on her hips and give him a lecture on morality. Instead she smiled and made his day.

"You know, if we were in a bar," she said, "I'd throw a drink right in your face." Then she smiled and made his day. "But under the circumstances, that's not such a bad idea."

Fitz-Hume took her arm, made a small bow in Millbarge's direction. "You will excuse us, won't you?" he said, turned, and led her away.

Millbarge blinked. It was a cliché, wasn't

it? The sort of thing they'd talked about in high school and now it was going to happen. The world was going to end with a bang and a whimper.

He looked at the Soviets. The shot-putt woman had followed Fitz-Hume's lead, grabbed the hand of the nearest man, and dragged him away.

Millbarge sighed. It was obvious who was going to get the girl. Of the two remaining crewmen, one was moon-faced, probably a Mongolian, pretty damned ugly.

The other was handsome, fit-looking, and tanned.

He glanced at the gorgeous creature he had fallen in love with. Already they had had quite a relationship. He'd seen her body. He'd knocked her unconscious. And in forty minutes, thanks to him, she would be a puff of charred dust.

Then something wonderful happened. The moon-faced crewman was winking at the handsome one. The handsome one pursed his lips. Moon-face smiled. Hand-in-hand they walked off together.

Which left the beauty.

He smiled tentatively at her. He had never been good at propositioning women. It had never worked in Washington and he knew he hadn't got any better at it in the last couple of days.

She smiled back, lowered her eyes, raised them again, giggled, and nodded. There was one tent left vacant. It was perfect. She was shy. But behind that little-girl smile lay . . . what? Millbarge didn't know.

But he was going to find out.

If it was the last thing he did.

— *Twenty-five* —

When the signal came up in red on his screen, the technician felt nothing. He saw it simply as a piece of information. Fear and panic could not grip him. Emotion had been suppressed in him by thorough training. To him, the Russian rocket was only a blip.

"SAC-COM confirms an outbound blip from Soviet Central Asia," he said.

"That's it," said Miegs. "It's on its way."

Ruby shivered at the tone of the man's voice. It was not fearful or even resigned. There was another word for it. *Satisfied*.

"Override all SAC alerts with error stand-down orders for ten minutes," said Sline.

"SAC override code entered," said a technician. He unlatched a red metal cover in the middle of his console. A red bulb pulsed like a heartbeat. Two keys waited in their locks.

Miegs and Sline looked at one another, nodded simultaneously. Together they reached for the keys, Miegs left-handed, Sline with his right. Together they turned the keys, and smiled.

In the blockhouse, the tip of the cannon throbbed and shuddered, the three prongs shaking, the whole thirty feet of it straining as if for take off, then it erupted, ejaculating a pulse of pure energy; iridescent, multicolored and crackling with static, a force created by the genius of mankind, unleashed for the first time in the history of the universe.

Faster than the speed of sound it zapped across the hundred yards in a rainbow blur, hit the deflector screen, and vanished for a moment. The wafers accepted it, drew it in. The screen pulsated, then, as programmed, the pulse was amplified a thousand times. The desert glowed green, then red, then blue, then the pulse was blasted out of the screen, a multicolored beam of energy in the shape of an arrow, hurled into the atmosphere. Fast. In a hurry. No time to waste.

It took three seconds to reach the first satellite, which, as programmed, welcomed it by expanding its deflector leaves, a thin mesh of wires, an electronic spider web, ready and waiting for the impact.

The pulse hit the deflector and bounced off.

General Miegs, when he had first had the

operation explained to him, had thought of a sporting allegory. It would be like a tennis match in space, a rally, with each stroke a perfect volley.

The first volley was perfect. A forty-five-degree angle.

The pulse, as programmed, zoomed high above the South Pacific while the second satellite's deflector screen opened to greet it. Meanwhile, halfway around the globe, the rocket reached the top of its trajectory.

Zap.

A perfect hit, another perfect volley and the pulse raced toward the third satellite.

Down below, the two generals waited. One more deflection and then . . . obliteration. A perfect defensive play. The world would be a safer place. The president would be able to look the critics and the skeptics in the eye and laugh.

The third satellite extended its aluminum arms. But not quickly enough. Somewhere, at some time down below, someone had blundered. Someone had not got his equations quite right. The mathematics were mistaken.

Unless the wafers unfolded faster, the pulse would not connect properly. There would be an inquiry. Heads would roll. The president would be unable to look the critics and the skeptics in the eye.

The pulse hit early. The wafers had not locked into position. It bounced off at sixty-five degrees, three degrees off course, and at that height it was disastrous. An inch up there was as good as a mile. It was as if the final player had mistimed a smash and sent the ball clear out of court. It was a miss. No appeal to a line judge.

A blunder of apocalyptic proportions.

The rocket began its descent toward the American continent. The pulse passed harmlessly under it. Headed for Mars.

Two hundred and thiry miles above California, an elderly satellite was on its two-thousandth orbit, spinning lazily, the words U.S. SPORTS, MOVIE & MUSIC NETWORK stenciled on its hull.

In a suburban house in Santa Monica, three teenage sisters were watching television. The room was a shrine to the music business. David Bowie competed for space with Michael Jackson, Cyndi Lauper with Prince.

Madonna had a wall all to herself.

On the screen the M-TV logo was reaching a climax. The rhythm guitarist hit a huge C chord.

The pulse hit the satellite.

The TV set exploded.

"Wow," said the sisters in perfect harmony.

In the bunker the technician's observation split the silence.

"Pulse beam failed to connect with target," he said

"Just what are you saying, soldier?" Sline asked.

"We missed it, sir."

"What?" said Miegs.

"We missed the rocket," the technician explained patiently. "It didn't work."

"It didn't work?" Sline repeated, his voice cracking. "Where did the pulse go?"

"I don't know, sir, but it definitely did not connect with the inbound traffic."

Miegs shook his head. "We missed. I can't believe it didn't work."

Keyes and Ruby looked at one another, Keyes suddenly feeling very old, Ruby fighting to retain control of his bowels.

"SAC-COM is rejecting all stand-down overrides," said the technician. "They are confirming full-alert status."

Ruby clenched his buttocks and got to his feet. The military had screwed up. Now he had to pick up the pieces. Fast.

"We'd better call the president," he said.

"We're not calling anyone," said Miegs softly.

Keyes stood up and glared at him. "What do you mean, we're not calling anyone? The president must know that this attack was not initiated by the Soviet Union."

Sline slowly shook his head. "We are prepared for this contingency," he said calmly.

Ruby couldn't believe what he was hearing. "What the hell do you intend to do?" he yelled, all control gone out of the window.

"You understand, sir"—the word *sir* a contemptuous hiss—"that we are responsible for the launching of a nuclear weapon against our own country!"

Miegs answered him, calmly, completely unruffled, in full control of himself. "No one outside of this command center has that information, gentlemen."

Keyes and Ruby gaped at him, then at Sline. They were speechless. Their brains simply couldn't cope with the messages they were receiving. Sline leaned forward and stared up at them, his hands clasped as if in prayer, as if about to deliver a sermon.

"When we commissioned the Schmectel Corporation to research this precise event-sequence scenario, it was determined that the continual stockpiling and development of our nuclear arsenal was self-defeating. A weapon unused is a useless weapon."

A technician interrupted him: "SAC-COM confirms all defense systems commitment ready."

Ruby began to shiver uncontrollably.

"We have verification," said a second technician. "The president is aboard the airborne command center now."

Sline nodded contentedly. "I'm sure it will be only a matter of minutes before the president commits to total release."

Then he did something that convinced Ruby and Keyes that he was totally mad.

He smiled.

"Jesus Christ," said Keyes, thinking of his childhood, of the old preacher who had preached what he regarded then as nonsense. Armageddon. The Book of Revelations was right after all.

"You see," Sline was explaining, "we had to show we had the technical capability and were determined. History demonstrates conclusively that naïve wishing for peace is the surest possible way to encourage an aggressor."

Ruby stood to his full height, tucked in his belly, and strove for a tone of authority in the face of this insanity. "I demand," he said, "that you place me in immediate communication with the president."

"Relax, Mr. Ruby," Miegs said soothingly. "This facility is more than adequately stocked for a comfortable seventeen months of below-ground existence. We'll be fine."

Keyes ignored him, concentrated on Sline. "By your actions, sir," he said, "you are risking the future of the human race."

Sline nodded in agreement, "To guarantee the American way of life," he said, "I am willing to take that risk."

—Twenty-six—

It had been unbelievable. The best ever. The more so because she didn't understand a word he had been saying to her. Millbarge had fantasized happily without need for censorship, and from the sound of her voice, she had been doing the same.

The tent had been a babble of bilingual dirty talk. Now it was over for the moment and she was nibbling his ear and he was wondering how long it would be until he was fit to start again, so that he could be talking to her again when the end of the world happened.

"It's only been a few minutes since I destroyed the world," he said to himself. "In another few minutes it will be all over. Such a short time to destroy a world. And to think

181

my guidance counselor said I'd never amount to anything."

Suddenly he sat up. A word had triggered a fragment of memory.

"Wait a minute," he said.

She nibbled his shoulder.

"Guidance."

She thought he meant something else. Went further down, tongue flickering.

"Source programmable guidance long-range rocket."

She grabbed him with both hands.

"Source programmable guidance," he said, and he was off, leaving her stranded and confused, hopping out of the tent, pulling on his pants, stumbling barefoot into the snow and yelling for the others.

"Up. Everyone up. Fitz-Hume. Comrades. There might be a way." •

Partially clad figures emerged blinking from the tents and gazed at him as if he had gone mad. Millbarge grabbed the arm of the leader. She squealed. He was hurting her and babbling in her face.

"You. Quick. Where's the instruction manual for this thing?"

She stared at him openmouthed as Fitz-Hume butted in.

"You had a tent?" he said admiringly, looking at the young woman as she came out, zipping herself up. Then: "What are you doing?" he asked Millbarge.

"I think we can recall it."

"Recall it? Like a defective Pinto?"

Millbarge ignored him and began explaining in Russian what he wanted the Soviets to do. As he spoke, they started running in all directions.

"Boyer," he said. "Get the Satscram sender. Fitz-Hume, grab a rock. Anything."

One of the Soviets was opening up a panel in the launcher, revealing a complex maze of wiring and circuitry. Another was climbing the erector arm, clutching a silver umbrella aerial.

Fitz-Hume watched all this in amazement, then found what he was looking for.

"Here's a rock," he said as Boyer rushed up to Millbarge with the Satscram terminal.

"What am I supposed to do with it?" Fitz-Hume asked.

"Smash that thing," Millbarge said, pointing to the scrambler. Fitz-Hume did as he was told. Ours not to reason why, he thought, as he battered it, hurting his thumb, bringing tears to his eyes. It was a solid piece of equipment. He smashed it again. And again until he had mangled it.

"Boyer," Millbarge shouted. "Start sending an override through their keyboard. Then send the launch sequence in reverse order."

She went to the console and did as she was told. Everyone was doing what Millbarge told them.

The Soviet with the aerial had reached the top of the erector arm now. He slipped.

They held their breaths as he dangled by one arm, then breathed in relief again as he found a grip, fixed the aerial in position, and gave the thumbs-up sign.

"Okay," said Millbarge. "I need the signal adjustment board to augment their sending selector."

The older woman gave him the piece of equipment he needed: a circuit board and two wires.

"It's too late," Boyer said. "It's probably all over."

"No," said Millbarge, furiously attaching wires to the board. "It's been sixteen minutes since it was launched. It would take that model at least twenty-five minutes to impact in North America. If I can bridge the adjustment and selection boards from our system into their selector, I can send the recall signal through our satellite network."

He held up two wires and motioned Fitz-Hume to come to him.

"Hold these together," he said. "You are the circuit bridge."

"What if I get a shock?" Fitz-Hume asked.

"Just don't let go, that's all."

He handed the wires over. Fitz-Hume grabbed them. Millbarge worked feverishly. Voltage passed through Fitz-Hume's body and he yelled. But he didn't let go. He couldn't.

"Oh shit," said Millbarge.

"What?" Fitz-Hume stammered, eyes bulging.

There was a crucial piece of equipment

missing. Millbarge looked all around him. "I need a . . . a . . . a . . ."

"A what?" said Fitz-Hume, teeth chattering in shock. "What? Bigger than a breadbox?" he coaxed. "Title of a movie? Title of a book?"

"A . . . a . . . a . . ."

The younger woman walked up to him, anxious to please. He snapped his fingers, grinned, leaned forward, and pulled a bobby pin from her hair.

"Got it," he said.

And jammed the pin into the launcher's electrical innards. A spark, a puff of smoke. Fitz-Hume dropped the wires and fainted.

The rocket was poised above Washington, D.C., and on course for its target. Then in its mechanical intestines, something rumbled. Electronic flatulence. Dials clicked and tumblers tumbled in response to Millbarge's instructions.

From its rear, a set of steering thrusters blasted into the heavens and slowly the rocket began to change direction.

Twin boosters spat fire and the rocket sped away from the planet, ever upward into the void.

It wasn't designed for such a maneuver. Slowly and inevitably the rocket began to self-destruct. The metal fatigued, crumpled, split. The warhead couldn't take the pressure and at eight miles high, it exploded.

In observatories all over the world, astron-

omers and space technicians watched awe-
struck as a new star was born, an awesome
fission-fusion burst in the region of Cassio-
peia. And they did not understand. They dealt
in celestial harmony and the laws of physics.
They weren't accustomed to seeing the sky
light up, right, as it were, on their doorstep.

Some of them broke a habit of a lifetime
and started praying.

In the bunker the stewards were preparing
for the hibernation, checking inventories
of food and drink and bedding and toilet
requirements.

Ruby and Keyes were slumped in their
seats, in shock, speechless, thinking of their
loved ones.

A technician turned away from his console. "General Miegs," he said. "SAC-COM
confirms destruction of the inbound at Zulu
three thousand hours."

"What about the rest of the inbounds?"
Miegs asked.

"There are none. Both U.S. and Soviet response chain are on full recall."

"Damn," said Sline. "Recall." It was a curse.
A six-letter obscenity.

He got to his feet, towering with rage, as a
message flashed on every screen:

SECURITY BREACH

They turned toward the door. It was sound-
proofed but not enough to muffle completely
the sound of gunfire. Then the door was

blasted open. Smoke filled the bunker. For a moment no one could see, but as the smoke cleared, they saw a crater where the door had been, and in the middle a major in the assault uniform of the U.S. Rangers surrounded by his men, their weapons aiming at them.

"Wait," said Keyes, showing the initiative that had gotten him to the top. "We don't know these men." He pointed to Sline and Miegs.

"Yes, we were kidnapped," Ruby said.

"Yes," said Keyes. "That's right. Kidnapped."

The major wasn't impressed. "Place them all under arrest," he said. "All of them."

four-second recesses for a short, for the busting from a spokesman on the American teams with some good news. The dasy are waiting to hear the chief's decision. The news should be good, but we are waiting to hear about what significant step forward may be being taken here in Geneva to help ease the tension that has been building up over the past few weeks. One has to hope that these disarmament talks

— Twenty-seven —

An old Ronald Reagan movie was playing coast to coast and Reagan was getting into a clinch with Doris Day when the network controller put his neck on the line and did a brave thing. He interrupted the clinch for a newsflash.

The scene was Geneva. A crowded hotel corridor, bustling with newsmen and women from all over the world.

Edwin Newman took his cue and talked directly to camera.

"As the disarmament talks continue here through closed sittings last night and on to this afternoon, a feeling of positive anticipation is shared by everyone in the press corps, all expecting to hear of a significant breakthrough in the negotiations.

"We are waiting now as this last twenty-

hour-session recesses, for a short, formal briefing from a spokesman on the American team,
we hope with some good word. The doors are
opening and I see the chief U.S. negotiator,
Emmett Fitz-Hume, emerging now."

Double doors were pushed open and Fitz-
Hume stepped out. He was wearing a five-
hundred-dollar suit and smiling a contented
smile, looking happily exhausted.

"Mr. Fitz-Hume," said Newman.

"Hi Ed," said Fitz-Hume cheerily.

"I'm sure everyone at home is most anxious to know how it's going in there."

"Well, Ed, we are at an extremely sensitive juncture now."

"Sensitive?" said Newman, frowning, looking concerned.

"Our discussions have surpassed limita-
tion guidelines and we are focusing not
merely on arms reductions. We are talking
at this point about nothing less than the
total dismantling and destruction of all ex-
isting nuclear stockpiles on both sides."

"That's extraordinary news indeed," said
Newman, happy with his scoop. "But do you
really think the Soviets would even consider
such a prospect?"

"It's true that they are extremely unpre-
dictable, Ed, but we are doing everything in
our power to structure the necessary com-
promises. Again I must stress the extremely
precarious balance which has been struck.
The slightest misperceived phrase or gesture

could upset everything we have achieved to date. Now, if you'll excuse me."

"Well, thank you, Mr. Fitz-Hume."

"Thank you, Ed," said Fitz-Hume, giving a cheery wave to the cameras and going back to the negotiating room.

Newman turned back to the camera. "Mr. Emmett Fitz-Hume, chief state-department negotiator, reentering what he has termed 'the sensitively balanced negotiations.'"

Inside, beer cans and vodka bottles were piled three feet high. On the negotiating table, a six-foot-square atlas of the world was covered in plastic rockets.

Fitz-Hume sat next to Boyer and winked at her, took a slug of beer and burped. Next to Boyer, the gorgeous Soviet crew woman sat on Millbarge's knee.

Opposite sat the other four Soviets, dressed for the occasion in ceremonial uniform and happily drunk.

"Shall we resume, Mr. Fitz-Hume?" said Boyer.

"Yes," he said, kissing her lightly on the ear. "Let us resume."

She reached over to the table, drew a card from a plastic container, and handed it to Millbarge, who dragged his face away from his woman for a moment and read aloud: "What Little Richard song was the title of a 1950s movie starring Jayne Mansfield?"

It wasn't fair. They didn't have the culture. They discussed it among themselves, frowning, trying to think.

Moon-face suggested "Great Balls of Fire" but he was outvoted. The handsome one wanted "Rip It Up." The woman went for "Good Golly Miss Molly."

A heated discussion, then a consensus.

"Good Golly Meess Molly," said the woman.

"Wrong," Millbarge whooped. "It was 'The Girl Can't Help It.' "

Gloom in the Russian camp. A great chorus of disappointment as Fitz-Hume leaned forward and swept red rockets off the map.

"Sorry, you lose Eastern Europe."

He kissed Boyer.

Millbarge's woman looked upset at the loss of Eastern Europe and so he tickled her ear. She smiled.

They kissed.

On TV all across the continental U.S.A. and beamed by satellite to Europe, Ronald Reagan was kissing Doris Day.

It was a very happy ending.

GREAT FILMS, GREAT BOOKS FROM SIGNET